THE DOG
IN THE HOLLOW

Will Lowrey

THE DOG IN THE HOLLOW

Copyright © 2022 by William C. Lowrey

This is a work of fiction. Names, characters, places, and incidents either are the product of the author's imagination or are used fictitiously. Any resemblance to actual persons, living or dead, events, or locales is entirely coincidental.

Editing by Lana Mowdy
Cover by Youness El Hindami
Formatting by The Book Khaleesi

Published by Lomack Publishing

www.lomackpublishing.com

ISBN 978-1-7329399-2-9 (Paperback)

First Edition

ALSO BY WILL LOWREY

Once in a Wild
The Animals v. Samuel Willis
Chasing the Blue Sky
Where the Irises Bloom
The Tenebrous Mind
Words on a Killing
Odd Robert
Simple Strategies for the Bar Exam

*For the ones who survived
and the ones who did not.*

"Come to the woods, for here is rest. There is no repose like that of the green deep woods. Sleep in forgetfulness of all ill."

~ John Muir ~

CHAPTER 1

At the crest of a gently sloping mountain where dark silhouettes of towering red spruce trees wavered against the fading azure sky, the late-summer sun sparkled and shimmered above the hollow below. A faint westerly breeze whispered across the mountain, and the waxy leaves of beech trees and sugar maples flittered on the wind.

Down in the hollow, where the trees gave way to a craggy, rocky pasture, Goose stirred at the end of his thick, iron chain. Night in the hollow was disquieting for the dogs imprisoned there.

He walked to the edge of his muddy clearing until the chain pulled taut against the rusted axle driven deep into the ground. His paws sank deep beneath the surface of a murky puddle, and he stood staring across the clearing toward a thin strand of mixed oaks. Straining forward on his chain and peering through the tree line, his eyes searched for the Man. Beneath his filthy buckskin fur, his frame was lean, and his ribs protruded visibly.

From the corner of his eye, he caught movement across the clearing and turned his head to look. Fifty yards away, Queen paced at the end of her chain; her eyes were upon him. Back and forth, she drifted through her dominion of mud. Her steps were fluid — almost elegant. In the long shadows that drew over the hollow, Goose could see the shimmer of her onyx eyes watching him. Although she paced at the far end of her chain, the metal was not pulled taut like Goose's; she knew every inch of the binding and expended no wasted effort straining against her own axle driven deep into the rocky ground. Back and forth she walked, watching him. There was something placid about her; she was a creature comfortable in her own skin, yet her eyes were those of a patient predator.

Goose's fur began to tremble, and he fought to suppress any outward signs of fear. Weakness did him no good here. His eyes scanned the horizon above the forest, longing for night to fall and shield her eyes with the shadows of darkness.

Beyond the stand of oaks, the familiar screeching of rusted hinges pierced across the hollow, and as one, the dogs turned on their chains to the sounds. Seven desperate, hungry mouths began to bark and whine, calling urgently for their once-daily meal. Beyond the trees, the thin metal door of the beige clapboard house slammed on its broken spring; the harsh sound quickly vanished beneath the din of hungry barking. In the distance, Goose could see the shape of a man step off the rotting front porch. His shadows cast long and menacing across the crumbling side of the old house with its paint peeling like cancerous scars.

Soon, the sound of rubber boots pounding impatiently through the muddy slop drew near. Goose tugged at the end of his chain, straining toward the sound. From the shadows of the trees, the Man approached, carrying a battered and dingy five-gallon bucket at his side. Though only middle-aged, the Man's face looked tired and haggard, and his mouth bore a sour, downward turn beneath a thick brown mustache. On his head, a tattered baseball cap contained unkempt wisps of dark hair.

When the Man reached Delilah, the closest, he stopped and lifted the bucket with both hands. She jumped on her hind legs, stretching at the end of the chain toward the bucket, but the Man kneed her harshly, sending her skittering across the soggy ground. She rose, her filthy white coat splashed with streaks of grime and mud. Unceremoniously, the Man turned the bucket and poured it into her metal bowl; hard kibble bounced and rattled noisily. Delilah dove her nose into the bowl, and Goose could see the muscles of her throat pulsing as she devoured the contents. After only seconds, she lifted her head, asking for more, but the Man was already gone.

Goose strained on his chain as the Man approached, his form barely more than a silhouette against the chalky sky. When he drew near, Goose inhaled his scent — the stale odor of cigarettes faintly masked by the harsh musk of body odor.

The Man stopped in Goose's puddle and lifted the bucket but did not pour. Goose stood there at the end of his chain, his mouth open wide, panting, but he did not bark or jump.

"Big day tomorrow," hissed the Man, staring down at Goose with a discerning gaze. "Got high hopes for you."

Then he tilted the bucket and poured a meager handful of kibble. As it rattled around, Goose stretched forward and buried his nose in the tattered metal bowl and gobbled greedily as the Man continued around the circle of dogs chained to the ground.

He stopped briefly at the next dog, Achilles, another buckskin male from Goose's litter. The dog barked hungrily at the Man as he approached and then pressed off the soft ground with his powerful legs, leaping until the chain pulled taut and slung him back to the muddy ground. Undeterred, Achilles sprang to his feet with an impressive nimbleness and leapt again, his paws flailing at the Man. The Man pushed his foot out and planted the heel of his boot in Achilles' pinkish underside, thrusting him backward. The dog hurtled into a blue barrel that served as a meager shelter, knocking it sideways. The Man scoffed with mild amusement.

"You'll get yours," he chided Achilles as he turned the bucket slightly and poured kibble into the bowl. Achilles was back on his feet, nose-down in the bowl as the Man turned and walked away.

The Man continued around the circle of dogs and stopped twenty yards away from Achilles. Seated there patiently in a filthy puddle sat Storm, her black coat melding with the shadows cast by the long trees that overlooked the hollow. Her mouth opened in a half-pant, and she looked calm and happy to see the Man as he approached. When he was near, she rose on all fours, and her tail whipped side to side. She seemed more eager to see the human than the food he brought. Storm stood there patiently and let him tilt the bucket until the kibble rattled around in the bowl. She watched him the whole time with her mouth open in what might pass to a human as a smile. The ribs on her narrow, muscled sides pulsated in and out. The Man finished pouring her food and continued on, never once acknowledging the dog. Only when he was several feet away did Storm step toward the bowl and begin to eat.

Queen circled on her chain as the Man approached. She moved effortlessly, gliding in smooth arcs back and forth across her muddy patch, just an inch short of pulling the chain taut. In her movements and manners, she spoke to the Man.

I am ready.

From across the craggy meadow, Goose could sense the Man's demeanor. He could feel the Man's spirits flutter and lift as he approached Queen. Thicker and more muscled than her sister, Storm, her sleek fur seemed to sparkle in the early dusk. Occasionally, the scant rays of sun that filtered through the trees into the hollow twinkled off her onyx eyes, which seemed to shine like jewels in this barren place.

The Man approached and stopped before her. He lowered his hand and softly stroked the crown of her head. Queen seemed unfazed, her demeanor never softening at the touch. She leaned forward and sniffed into the bucket dispassionately. From across the clearing, Goose could see the tendons rippling in her thickly-muscled thighs. On her chest, long veins ran vertically down her shoulders; her skin was tight and lean.

As her head slipped past the bucket, she scanned the clearing. At once, the others looked away or rested timidly on their haunches, their deference to Queen apparent. Her eyes fell on Goose, who stood there, subconsciously staring at the bucket beside her, still hungry. The sharp, pointed remnants of Queen's ears pricked upright, and her dark eyes seemed to bore right through him. Suddenly, his hunger vanished, and Goose looked away, circling back toward his blue barrel.

After a few moments, the Man continued around the circle of chained dogs, feeding the last two. First came Zeus, a stocky, well-muscled dog, who seemed impassive as the Man approached. His body was conditioned to subsist with minimal food, and the sight of the bucket did not arouse him. Zeus's fleshy forearms and snout stood out against his reddish-white coat, much of the fur long since replaced by the scars of countless punctures.

And finally, on the far side of Delilah, was Rocket, her wiry black brindle frame barely visible in the shadows of the tall trees. As the Man approached, she darted forward on her chain, poking her nose at him, and then lurched backward. She was lean and her mannerisms sudden and hectic. The Man stopped at her bucket and poured a small amount of kibble into her bowl, and she stayed several feet back, her narrow frame hunkered low to the ground. Then her head poked forward, sniffing at the air.

When the Man finished, he shook the bucket, and the last remnants of food rattled against the hard plastic. He turned the bucket and dumped it into Rocket's bowl and, without ceremony, pivoted and trudged away from the circle of hungry dogs toward the edge of the forest. There, in the shadows of the mountain, where the broad-leaved hardwoods gave way to the spruce-fir forest, rested a decrepit mobile home. The drab white, corrugated metal was trimmed with a faded powder blue that seemed to intrude on the hollow and disfigure its natural beauty.

The Man sloshed across the muddy ground until he reached the rusting shell. Goose rested back on his haunches and watched him closely as his boots pounded on the thin metal stairs set against the entrance. When he reached the top, Goose could hear the old knob squeak, and the door opened, revealing the innards of the structure like a gaping black maw. The Man stepped inside, and the door closed behind him. Soon, through the seams in the thick sheets of cardboard plastered across the broken windows, Goose saw a yellow light emanating from the shadowy husk of the mobile home there at the forest's edge.

Across the yard, Queen pulled at her chain and

whimpered, tugging toward the dingy structure, longing to follow the Man. Nearby, Zeus responded to Queen's movement and stretched forward on his chain, his muscles pulsing under the tension. At the movement, Queen turned toward him and lunged, her teeth gnashing violently in the air, restrained only by the metal axle driven deep into the ground. Zeus responded in turn, lowering his head close to the ground and pulling hard on his front legs until his thick, leather collar dug deep into his neck. Froth bubbled from the side of his mouth, and the two dogs snapped and threatened at the ends of their chains, unable to meet.

Across the yard, Goose lowered his head and pressed it against his chest. Their anger was foreign to him. Although he had lived at the end of this chain for over a year, he had not yet lost himself to the madness as some of the others had. The anger in Queen and Zeus was something entirely unknown to him. Deep inside them, something troubling brewed — something perverse and primal, unlike anything he felt within himself. He sensed it in some of the others but not to the same degree as these two. Though Storm was quiet and subdued, he had watched her lash out on occasion, the anger spilling forth suddenly and without warning. Goose had seen Storm when she returned from the blue and white trailer. An angry spirit seemed to roil within her; her eyes were wild and crazed as she returned to the chain.

Goose knew the same sickness lay within Rocket; in fact, it seemed to consume her. The whole world was Rocket's enemy, and she cowered and hid from the smallest threats. The winds and rains tormented her and drove her to the back of the blue barrel laid sideways, where she shivered in the blackness. On nights when the raucous cars and trucks with their bright lights would roll up beyond the stand of trees near the house, Goose could see her shivering. When the summer storms rolled across the mountain and the thunderclouds swirled dark and angry, she dug deep into her moldy straw. Yet when other dogs were near, she was alive. The Man often took her to the blue and white trailer, and she followed him on the short leather leash, digging her paws feverishly into the ground to follow the scent of another dog already within. And when the doors of the crumbling mobile home closed and the silence drew across the forest, Goose could hear the horrible sounds from deep within.

Across the hollow, the lights flickered behind the cardboard, and blackness filled the seams once more. The door creaked open, and Goose could just see the silhouette of the Man in the doorway. He pulled the door shut and stomped down the stairs. Zeus and Queen stood silent at attention, waiting for him to take them to the trailer. But without the slightest look in their direction, the Man strode along the line of trees, turned down a worn path leading to the old beige house, and faded into the infringing blackness.

In the distance, Goose heard the bucket drop on the ground, the metal handle rattling against the plastic. A moment later, the metal screen door of the house opened with a sharp screech and then clattered shut behind the man. The hollow grew silent once more.

Above him, the last remnants of blue sky had faded to a dusty gray, and only faint wisps of the dying sun's rays rose above the tips of the spruce that ringed the mountaintop. In the burgeoning darkness, the dogs sat or milled, resigned to the drudgery of another night of misery. Beside him, Achilles nosed at his empty bowl, flipping it over in the mud. He dipped his head as if waiting for kibble to appear magically, and when there was none, he laid down in the mud and rested his head on his paws. On the other side of him, Delilah whimpered, discontent.

Across the clearing, Goose watched Rocket's wispy tail vanish into the shadows of her blue barrel, and he saw it wiggle as the wiry dog curled into her rotten straw. In the darkness, across the yard, though he could not see her black shape merged as one with the shadows, he could feel Queen's onyx eyes upon him, and he knew she stood there like a statue, watching and waiting.

As the last vestiges of dusk turned to an inky black, Goose sniffed once at his bowl, assuring himself he had left no morsels behind. Hopeless, he turned and lowered his head, stepping into his blue barrel. The straw was wet and old, and the pungent, foul smells stung his nostrils. He crawled to the back of the barrel and curled himself into a ball, his eyes just raised above his hind legs so he could stare into the blackness of the hollow.

Soon, he closed his eyes and gave himself to the boredom. In the depths of the forest, somewhere up the dark mountainside, rose the *yip yip* of a lonesome coyote followed by a long, quavering howl that seemed to echo across the mountain.

CHAPTER 2

Above the hollow, the dusty gray morning sky faded to powder blue, and the sun inched its way above the treetops, illuminating the barren yard dotted with blue barrels. From each barrel, a rusted metal chain spilled out, their ends fastened to iron rods driven deep into the mountain soil.

Soon, Goose could hear the discordant, dull clanking of the chains being dragged just outside his dingy lair. He lifted his head from the moldy straw and gazed out at the world.

In the dim light of morning, he could see Queen standing at the end of her chain, staring stoically toward the old beige house just beyond the line of trees. To her right, Zeus lay on the muddy ground, just before his barrel, his head tilted backward, his eyes drawn tight to slits, and his nose searching for scents on the morning air. Beside Zeus, Rocket cowered in the back of her barrel, only the glimmer of her frightened eyes visible from across the yard.

For most of the morning, the dogs languished or paced in the yard, alternating between the paltry shade of their barrels and the sunlit mud that baked beneath the cloudless sky. Occasionally, Goose perked his ears at the sounds of the Man toiling near the house. The screen door creaked and slammed repeatedly throughout the day as he came and went, unseen beyond the trees.

In the afternoon, the Man strode toward the yard, and the dogs rose as one to greet him, awaiting their scant morsels of kibble, but there was none. The Man walked past them, empty-handed, glancing only briefly in their direction, and headed toward the old mobile home at the edge of the forest. The door to the dilapidated structure opened and then closed as he vanished into the belly of its rusted husk, the thin metal rattling behind him.

Beside Goose, Achilles whimpered softly and then lifted his head and barked balefully into the depths of the forest. Goose turned toward his brother and their eyes met briefly; he could see the hunger within him. Achilles lowered his head as if embarrassed to have succumbed momentarily to the pangs of hunger. From across the yard, Queen and Zeus looked on, emotionless, their bodies long since adapted to the regiment. Goose studied them from across the yard. They seemed eager.

After several minutes, the door flapped open, banging into the side of the mobile home, and the Man pounded down the metal steps, his eyes cast toward the ground. He seemed to walk with purpose past the yard and back toward the edge of the tree line. As he passed, his eyes glanced toward the dogs once more and seemed to land briefly on Queen then shifted and fell on Goose.

His gaze sent a shiver up Goose's spine, like a man measuring the worth of his living property. Goose turned away toward the blue barrel, but he could feel the eyes upon him still as the Man's feet carried him further and further away. Once more, Achilles whimpered and barked at the Man, and once more, he ignored them and vanished beyond the trees and into the old house.

Soon, dusk began to draw over the hollow, and the wispy tendrils of the tall trees seemed to grow like giant claws, looming larger and larger. Above him, the sky was indifferent — barren of sun or moon as if trapped in some purgatory between the phases of day and night.

Then, as one, the dog's ears perked, and they rose to their feet with a chorus of barks and a cacophony of chains. The sound of tires crunching on the scattered rocks of the old dirt logging road that wound its way to the edge of the house cut through the stillness. The dogs leaned forward on their chains, sensing the approaching presence.

Across the yard, Queen stared through the trees to the corner of the house. Goose could feel the unmistakable power of the aura that emanated from her.

Soon, yellow lights cut across the yard, slashing from one side to the next as the dark silhouette of a pickup truck emerged from the distant forest and turned sharply before the house. The sound of gears shifting echoed across the yard, and the truck's silhouette bucked briefly and then came to a rest, its lights illuminating the scarred blemish of a house for a moment and then flickering off until there was only blackness.

Goose could sense the presence of a dog somewhere in the rear of the truck, hidden behind a flaking plastic camper shell. Though the dog made no sounds, her presence was unmistakable. Her spirit was strong and determined.

Then, the sound of rubber tires rose once more, and a second pair of lights flickered across the hollow as another vehicle pulled up beside the pickup truck and its lights went dim. Goose heard doors opening on the two vehicles and the voices of men talking indecipherably somewhere in the blackness.

The old screen door of the house creaked again, and he could sense the Man step out. Soon, his voice greeted the others and they spoke, their tones boisterous and jovial. After a moment, the cover of blackness that crept over the hollow was again disturbed by the flashing of lights as a third vehicle approached and then a fourth and a fifth. Before long, the silhouettes of nearly a dozen vehicles filled the chalky sky beyond the trees, and the voices of many men rose within the hollow. Through the men's raucous conversation, Goose could hear them — the desperate barking of many dogs hidden in crates and cages in the back of trucks and cars. Their strange, anxious voices seeped through the cracks of windows and camper shells and filled the hollow with electric energy.

Queen and Zeus sensed the dogs and seemed to tense at the ends of their chains. In the darkness, they rested silently alert. Goose strained his eyes into Rocket's barrel and could see the glimmer of her eyes darting back and forth from the blackness. The entire day, she had not emerged from the barrel, but now she seemed awake and alive at the sounds.

By the time the vehicle lights had all gone dim and the crunching of tires on the winding road fell silent, the cloak of inky night had drawn above the sky and the dogs rested anxiously at the ends of their chains. Above them, the distant stars twinkled wondrously.

THE DOG IN THE HOLLOW

Soon, the sound of many footsteps pounding to the end of the craggy road gave way to their soft thudding on the soggy ground. The beams of a half-dozen flashlights splayed across the yard from one dog to the next and then turned and illuminated the old trailer. Behind the lights, Goose could see the patchy silhouettes of men moving through the darkness, talking in low tones to each other. A chill ran up his spine, and he hunkered low along the ground in the black night as if he might hide from them.

As they turned their lights to the trailer, the yard grew black again. Delilah barked at the rear of the men as they passed, and Goose could hear Queen rattling on her chain, moving eagerly toward the Man as they approached the distant trailer. Then, he heard the thin metal door open, and the faint light from the trailer broached the darkened yard, illuminating Zeus standing alert at the end of his chain, his muscles rippling beneath the pale glow. Across the yard, Goose saw the lights briefly flicker across Rocket's glowing eyes; she remained tucked deeply in the depths of her barrel.

He watched the men enter the trailer, one by one. There was almost a dozen of these strangers; the brims of their baseball hats, the distant burning embers of their stale cigarettes, and the bitter words that spilled from their lips were all he knew of them.

WILL LOWREY

The door of the trailer closed, and the light faded, turning the yard to darkness once more. Only thin slits of yellow light peered through the gaps in the cardboard. Goose lay on the ground, his chin to the mud, and he lifted his ears, straining to listen into the night. Only the muffled vibrations of strange voices from deep within the mobile home carried across the hollow.

To his left, a car door opened, and he jerked suddenly at the sound. Against the light, he saw two men left standing by the vehicles, talking calmly. Their voices carried and vanished into the woods. Goose could still sense the presence of the dogs in the cars that the other men had left behind. Occasionally, one would bark anxiously, and one of the two men would rap on the window of a camper or the metal door of a vehicle and silence the dog.

After a long while, the door to the trailer opened, and the light poured out into the yard again. Zeus remained stoic and vigilant — a statue guarding the night. The sound of footsteps thumped down the metal stairs, and a man walked hurriedly to the vehicles, passing beside the stand of mixed oaks without a word. When he reached the cars, he exchanged words with the two men who had remained, and then Goose heard the creaking of a tailgate. He could sense the dog now, no longer hidden from the night air by the vacuum of the vehicle. His nose twitched as he could smell her — raw, powerful, and eager. She carried with her a strange presence of muted anticipation. He could hear her feet jump from the rear of the vehicle and land nimbly on the muddy road. In the distance, the faint jingling of a chain carried through the night as she shook herself, releasing tension from the long journey to this place.

Then, the man from the trailer began to walk with her and she followed, her silhouette trotting obediently beside him. The man hurried toward the trailer, and as he passed within yards of Zeus, the stocky red and white male pulled tight on his chain, straining toward the dog with his powerful legs. Even in the faint slivers of light that spilled into the hollow between the gaps in the cardboard windows, Goose could see the thick muscles rippling on his hind legs. As the man approached, the door to the trailer opened once more, and the light spilled out. Goose could see the new dog, a dingy white female. A thick leather collar gripped her taut, muscular neck, and her sinewy legs stretched out for the metal stairs and scurried upward, disappearing behind the closing door.

For several long moments, the yard was silent, and then the door opened once more. In the light, Goose saw the familiar shadow of the Man. He stood at the top of the stairs, gazing out into the yard. His eyes turned to his left and fell purposely on his champion — Queen. She stood obediently waiting for him.

The Man stepped quickly down the stairs toward Queen, and slowly, her erect tail began to wag tentatively back and forth; even her apparent delight was carefully and methodically controlled. When he reached her, he grabbed her by the collar, and Goose could hear a jingling of keys across the yard. The Man fumbled briefly with the keys in the light of the open doorway as another man stood inside the trailer, only his arm extended outward to the yard to hold the door. After a moment, Goose heard the clinking of the metal lock, and Queen was free from her chain, her thick collar gripped tightly by the Man, who led her back toward the steps. She trotted beside him like the finest show horse, graceful and proper, her movements careful yet fluid. Her claws clicked across the metal stairs, and soon, the door flapped shut behind her, and the voices of the brash men faded into muffled noise behind the thin metal walls of the trailer.

At the slamming of the door, Goose rose to his feet. A chill ran down the length of his back, and the gritty, buckskin hairs on his spine stood on end. His heart began to pound, and the remaining dogs in the yard — except for Zeus — seemed to tremble in anticipation of some grave event. Across the yard,

THE DOG IN THE HOLLOW

Zeus edged closer to the trailer, pulling taut on the chain, his nose sniffing hard toward the door as if beseeching it to open and allow him entry.

In the darkness, the muted sounds beyond the trailer walls grew and seemed to push brusquely through the cracks in the fragile metal seals. Then, they rose to shouts, and Goose shivered at the sudden sound of two objects colliding. The trailer seemed to rumble on its rotted skids, and the roars of the men grew louder. Behind the slits of light that shone through the cardboard windows, Goose could see movement— the dark shadows of men passing back and forth and moving about the trailer. He craned his ears and pressed into the night with his senses, and then he could hear it — the sound of two dogs engaged in mortal combat.

Again and again, the trailer seemed to shake and rumble. The men hollered and yelled vigorously. Goose's senses stretched far into the void so that he could almost hear them now, barely muted beyond the thin walls. Occasionally, the enraged growl or vicious snapping of a dog permeated the walls and reached his ears.

Zeus began to whimper and occasionally released a shrill whine as he thrust against his chain toward the trailer. Far in the corner of her barrel, Rocket curled tight, but Goose could see her shimmering eyes in the faint light — they burned with an anxious fever that seemed to await release. To his right, Achilles paced around and around, occasionally grumbling in unfocused tension at the sounds around him. Next to him, Goose could barely see Storm's shadow resting on her haunches, her dark eyes focused intently on the trailer.

For a brief moment, the rumbling of the trailer seemed to subside, and the old metal structure grew still, yet inside, Goose could hear the men's voices talking hurriedly and excitedly. Then once more, the trailer shook as the two dogs collided. Goose could hear a violent snarl, and he knew it was Queen. Her voice was strong and vigorous, and Goose could tell that she was in her element. Again, he heard Queen snarl as the gnashing of teeth echoed through the thin walls of the trailer. Finally, the trailer grew still, and in the depths of his heart, Goose could feel a life depart the hollow, and the cold vacuum of death seemed to emanate from within the metal shell. The raucous noises of the men settled and dimmed to a steady hum of conversation.

He stared at the door, entranced and afraid, and waited for it to open. Then it did. The deep yellow lights of the trailer spilled into the yard. Zeus pulled taut on his chain, stretching forward. The silhouette of a man appeared at the door. He stepped backward, hunched over as if dragging something behind him. His feet thumped on the metal steps, and then the body of the dingy white dog spilled out behind him, bouncing grotesquely on the metal stairs as he dragged her by her rear legs. Zeus stopped his whimpering as he digested the scene. The sight of the corpse stalled even Zeus's eagerness for a moment.

As the man dragged the dog's corpse down the last few steps, he turned and began to pull her across the yard toward the logging road. Then, another shadow appeared just beyond the doorway and called to him.

"Leave her over by the trees. I'll give her to the buzzards tomorrow," called the Man in his familiar voice.

Goose peered into the doorway, and the shadow turned to a silhouette as the Man began to step down the metal stairs, his right hand clenched on Queen's collar as he led her down to the ground. In the faded yellow light, Goose could see the fresh scars on her face. A jagged tear ran diagonally across her snout, and blood spilled to the ground. The white patch on her chest was streaked with crimson stains. As she stepped down the stairs, she walked gingerly, favoring her right leg. Her mouth was open in a pant, and Goose could sense the pulsing excitement of her spirit.

The Man walked her quickly back toward her

metal axle driven into the ground and reached down, fastening her thick chain to her collar. The unnatural clinking of the metal lock stirred in the now-quiet night, and she turned to face him. He paused for a moment and bent over her, wiping the blood from her snout with his hand until it dripped in a large puddle on the soggy ground.

The Man gave her a wan smile, and she locked eyes with him. Then without anything more, he turned and walked back to the trailer as she looked after him.

"That one's a beast," said a twanging voice from the silhouette of a man in a baseball cap standing at the entrance to the trailer.

"That's my girl," said the Man, his tone chipper, as he lowered his head and stomped up the stairs into the trailer.

Goose watched the man near the tree line drag the corpse of the white dog a few more feet, and then he released his grip on her legs, and they fell limply to the ground, her body consumed in the blackness before the trees. The man's silhouette turned and headed back toward the trailer. The tiny orange flame of a lighter flickered in the distance and lit the end of a cigarette into a glowing ember.

Goose turned and looked back across the yard to Queen. She rested on her stomach, licking at a series of punctures along her front legs. Next to her,

THE DOG IN THE HOLLOW

Zeus whimpered and pressed once more toward the door held open by the man in the baseball cap. The other man returning from the woods stepped into the light, and Goose strained his eyes to see him. Long, greasy black hair flowed over his shoulders. He grasped the single metal rail of the rickety steps with his wiry, sleeveless arm and pulled himself up into the trailer, tossing the burning cigarette to the ground in a single motion as he did.

From the belly of the trailer, Goose could hear the men talking loudly, their voices bellowing into the yard through the open door. Then, another man stepped to the door, his hulking frame blocking the yellow light and casting a long shadow across the yard, engulfing Zeus, who stood nearby.

The man turned over his shoulder and called back into the trailer, "Goin' to get Rebel." Then he stepped hard down the metal stairs, purposely skipping a step and landing hard enough that the ground seemed to shiver as he landed. He passed through the square of light cast by the door and moved into the blackness around the yard.

"Better hope your young one is game, Virgil!" he bellowed behind him.

In the doorway, the Man appeared once more; Goose recognized his silhouette. "I believe he is!" yelled the Man in return. Goose could hear a challenge in his tone. Then, Goose felt the Man's eyes scan across the yard and fall upon him. Those eyes bored into his chest, and his heart began to race. At the top of the metal stairs, the Man stood there, undeniably looking right at him. Though Zeus clawed at the dirt and whined for the Man just feet away, his cold gaze looked above the battle-worn dog and rested only on Goose.

The Man stepped down the stairs and strode across the yard, brushing Zeus on the crown of his head gently as he passed. He walked straight across the soggy ground. As he approached, Goose could smell his musky odor mixed with stale cigarettes and alcohol. Inside, Goose fought his emotions. The Man's approach usually meant food and some attention, yet tonight, he could tell the Man had other intentions, and it scared him to his core. Goose hunkered low into the ground and tucked his head away from the Man.

He stopped above Goose, casting a long shadow across his worn patch in the yard. "Don't you do me wrong now," he said to the dog. His voice was bitter, and his lips were twisted in a malignant scowl.

Then, the Man pulled the keys from his pocket, and the clanking of the metal seemed to thunder in Goose's ears as he hunkered low. In the faint light from the trailer door, he saw the glimmer of the copper key, and the Man pressed it into the padlock attached to Goose's neck. Then he heard the faint click that meant he was free. He felt the knobby bones of the Man's knuckles press into the side of his neck as the Man dug his hand beneath his collar and tugged at it.

Obediently, Goose rose to his feet. He wobbled unsteadily on his legs, and the Man pulled him forward, moving him into the light. He leaned over Goose, and the Man's rank breath swept across his sensitive nose. "Don't you let me down, you hear me?" he threatened, emphasizing each word ominously. Then the Man rose and began to pull Goose forward across the yard toward the trailer.

From the corner of Goose's eyes, he could see Queen rise to her feet as they passed just out of reach of her chain. He glanced at her from the corner of his eye. The bloody gash deep into her snout glistened in the dim yellow light from the trailer, and he saw something in her eye, something different than her usual intensity. It seemed like pity.

The Man pulled Goose along the yard, and the buckskin dog stepped quickly along beside him until he reached the step. Behind him, he could hear Zeus pulling on his chain, the metal links rattling and buckling with his thrusts. In the doorway, the figure in the baseball cap stepped aside, and the

Man pulled Goose up the stairs. His feet splayed and slipped on the metal steps, and he nearly fell sideways, but the Man yanked his collar and heaved him into the trailer. His long claws landed on the slick linoleum, and he slid headlong into the thin faux wood wall of the trailer, his paws leaving streaks in the puddles of blood that were splashed across the floor.

"I don't think that one's gonna do so good 'gainst Rebel," chortled the man with the baseball cap as he gestured at Goose. "I think you 'bout to have one less dog in this yard, Virgil," he scoffed.

Virgil hovered over Goose as he scrambled to his feet, fighting to gain his footing on the slick floor. Finally, he managed to stand. The darkness of Virgil's shadow loomed over him.

"Nah, he'll do just fine," said the Man, reaching down to grasp Goose's collar and pulling him deeper into the trailer.

Goose lifted his head and stretched his eyes as far as he could. Several feet ahead, a short plywood wall ran perpendicular across the width of the trailer. On the other side of the wall, he could see the crusted, matted shag of an old brown carpet spread flat across the floor covering the middle of the trailer and set between a second piece of plywood that formed a wall on the far side — the pit.

THE DOG IN THE HOLLOW

Just beyond the far wall, a small group of men milled and chattered among themselves, their eyes raising to study Goose as the Man dragged him closer to the pit. Their vile looks and harsh words seemed to fill the small trailer with a dark, turbulent cloud. Goose's heart began to race as the Man dragged him closer to the low, wooden wall. Just beyond, he could smell the terse scent of fresh blood on the shag carpet mingling with the stale scent of mildew and cheap beer.

"That one don't wanna fight, Virgil!" a pot-bellied man with a greasy white beard yelled from beyond the pit.

"Awww, shit. I got my money on Rebel!" bellowed a stocky, younger man, his sun-weathered skin and dark tattoos visible beneath a rumpled collared shift that flopped open as he hooted and gestured theatrically with his arms.

The Man bent down and placed his arms under Goose and lifted him into the pit. Tentatively, Goose set his paws down on the carpet — the texture was strange and foreign. The Man stood beside him in the pit as Goose pawed at the ground unsteadily, gauging the texture of the surface. He dipped his head low and looked up with his eyes, scanning the crowd. His tail tucked slightly beneath him, he began to sniff at the dingy carpet.

The Man bent over him, and Goose raised his

head as if he were meeting a kindly gesture, but he knew better. The Man straddled him and began to pull and tug at his thick collar. The leather dug into Goose's neck as the Man worked to unfasten the rusted steel buckle. Finally, the buckle released, and the tight leather strap gave way. Goose felt a rush of vigor when the collar released from his neck; he suddenly felt lighter and more alive. Slowly, his tail began to wag from side to side, and he stepped forward and began sniffing at the wooden wall that separated him from the boisterous men, who swilled their beer and leered down at him, their words echoing off the walls of the metal trailer.

Then, Goose heard the sound of footsteps rushing up the metal stairs — unmistakably, a man and a dog. He tensed and turned toward the entrance. A long shadow cast across the opening of the door, and once again, the man in the baseball cap stepped aside. As he did, the hulking man stepped into the trailer, panting as great pools of sweat dripped from his reddish beard and stained his tattered gray t-shirt with dark streaks. His thick arm was stretched forward like a pale, freckled tree trunk, clutching tightly a short leather leash attached to the thick collar of a tightly muscled chocolate brown dog. The dog stepped forward into the trailer. His moss-colored eyes searched the room intensely, and his body seemed to tremble with a barely bridled excitement.

"God damn, Rebel is ready to kill something!" hooted the stocky man behind Goose. Goose felt a splash of beer on his coat as the man gestured drunkenly in excitement.

Rebel took a step forward into the trailer, and his gaze fell on Goose, standing in the pit, clamped tightly between the Man's legs. His tiny black pupils seemed to bore into Goose like needles as he stretched forward. A low rumble brewed within his belly, and the muscles that stretched up his front legs bulged grotesquely. The burly man pulled back on the leash, and Rebel slid backward on the linoleum.

"You ready, Virgil?" said the man in the baseball cap as he let go of the door and it flapped closed behind Rebel.

The Man leaned down and placed his palms on either side of Goose's face and leaned over him. Goose was conflicted inside. The trailer swirled with turmoil and death. The boisterous yelling of the men behind him swirled and roiled in his head, and a part of him wanted to hunker down and cower in the corner. Yet, deep inside, he could feel the anger stirring within him at the menacing dog that leered at him with serpent eyes from just beyond the short, wooden wall.

"You better do me right," said the Man, staring

into Goose's eyes. He crouched down behind him and wrapped his right arm around Goose's chest, holding him tight against his body. "We're ready," he said, nodding toward the man in the baseball cap, who stepped over the low wall and entered the carpeted area.

"Let's do it," said the man.

The burly man tightened his grip on the leash, and Rebel pulled toward the wooden wall, bounding over in one short leap. The big man yanked back hard on the leash, and Rebel slammed into the wall. The wood shivered. Then, the man stepped over the wall and crouched beside Rebel, pressing the dog against his body as he unfastened the collar and leash. He looked up and nodded at the man in the hat.

The man in the hat glanced at Rebel and then again at Goose and raised his arm in the air and held it. Goose's heart raced in his chest, and his mind spun. He glanced over Rebel at the door, and his eyes quickly scanned the tiny trailer. There was no escape.

"Fight's on!" said the man in the hat as he chopped his arm downward. As he did, the burly man released his grip on Rebel. Goose felt the Man's arm slide from around his chest, and he could sense him stepping away over the rear wall.

Rebel was across the pit before Goose had his

feet under him. The brown dog shot at Goose like a blur, his head low like a battering ram. Just as he drew near, all Goose could do was shift his weight sideways to avoid the head-on collision. As he did, Rebel opened his jaws, and Goose could see the flash of his white canines just as they sank into the side of his neck. The pain ripped through Goose, sending sharp daggers through the length of his body. He staggered back into the wooden wall, and Rebel was on him with his full weight, his teeth digging into the soft flesh of his neck. Goose's legs buckled, and he began to fall, but something in him made him fight to keep his feet. He stretched out with his left front paw and braced himself. Then he twisted his head and stretched toward Rebel's exposed flank, desperate to free himself from the dog's grip. As he stretched, he could feel Rebel's teeth digging deeper into his flesh, and he could hear the snarls and feel the spittle of the other dog, his face only inches away. Goose stumbled again and then stretched with all he could muster and caught a piece of Rebel's flank with his teeth.

That seemed to enrage Rebel as he released the grip on Goose's neck and started to climb on his back, trying to topple him. His teeth gnashed downward at Goose as he spun to avoid being spilled on his side. As he did, Goose fell, crouching his legs to brace himself. Sensing the separation,

Goose moved to the corner of the pit, gaining distance from the other dog.

Rebel was back to his feet in a flash, charging once more into Goose. This time, as he neared, he lifted his front paws, propelling himself forward at Goose's face, his teeth gnashing in the air. Instinctively, Goose met him in the air, thrusting forward with his rear legs. Their bodies clashed violently, jaws snapping, teeth cracking as they each sought a vulnerable spot. Rebel pressed forward with his front paws, and Goose lost his footing, tumbling over to his side. Rebel was on him again, his teeth sinking deep into the other side of his neck. He shook his head, and Goose could feel his flesh tearing. He kicked desperately with his legs to free himself. Once more, Rebel snarled and shook his head violently. Goose wailed, and a dark shroud seemed to grow at the corner of his vision as he began to lose consciousness.

Just then, he heard the Man in the distance. "That's it!" he shouted. The disappointment in his voice was unmistakable.

"Pickin' up!" shouted the man in the baseball cap.

Goose's vision began to shift in and out of focus. He could feel the blood pooling in the side of his mouth, and he could hear himself panting. He could no longer feel the pain of Rebel's teeth sunk deep in his flesh, but he could feel the dog release, and he could smell the sweat of the burly man as he lifted Rebel off the ground. The hooting of the men beyond the far wooden wall swirled into a deep, indecipherable baritone that seemed to pound in his ears.

As he lay prone on the ground, the wisps of brown carpet just before his eyes faded in and out of focus, like giant trees on the distant ridge of the mountaintop on days when the thick clouds shrouded the sun. He could smell the familiar scent of the Man, and he could see his boots before him. He felt himself being lifted off the carpet, and he heard the creaking hinges on the trailer door. Then, the night was upon him, and all around was the blackness of the hollow. Above, the moon flashed like a broken bulb in his fading consciousness as the Man carried him across the yard. He felt his broken body drop heavily on the soggy mud, and he could smell the familiar mold of the straw in his blue barrel.

Just above him, the Man spoke, and his words were harsh and cruel. He heard the metal clasp of the lock being fastened to his collar, and he felt the peculiar cold of a gentle breeze that blew across his open, exposed wounds. Soon, the world went black.

CHAPTER 3

The morning sun climbed the sky above the mountains and showered the hollow with warmth. Below, Goose began to stir in his subconscious. Splayed in a hideous heap before his blue barrel, the young dog had not moved since his unceremonious dumping the night before, save for the shallow, ragged breaths that caused his protruding ribcage to pulsate grotesquely. Throughout the night and morning, Achilles had drawn near on his own chain; the last vestiges of brotherhood, suppressed but not completely obliterated by this forsaken place, stirred him with concern for his brother. Yet, no matter how many times Achilles barked or clawed at the muddy ground between them, Goose would not move.

Now, the incessant buzzing of the fat black horse flies that gathered near his open wounds seemed to stir his mind to consciousness. Slowly, the shroud of darkness began to recede. Goose could feel the pinprick legs of the tiny insects parading up and down the raw edges of the gruesome tears in his neck. Then, he felt the warmth of the sun's rays as they soaked into his filthy coat. Eyes closed, he extended his tongue, subconsciously lapping for moisture. When he did, the pain of broken teeth tore through his body, and his eyes shot open. He howled a woeful moan and tried vainly to lift himself from the ground but simply flopped limply on his side.

Achilles let out a shrill bark and scratched at the ground. Goose could hear his brother's chain clattering; he sounded so distant. Slowly, Goose rolled himself upright. The horse flies buzzed angrily and scattered but stayed near, as they knew the dog was weak. Goose stared ahead, and before him, the deep green of the forest seemed to wiggle and vibrate as he struggled to focus. He blinked his eyes, and his head lowered; he was almost too weak to keep himself upright. In the depths of his spirit, he knew he must not give in to the darkness, and he willed himself to rise. Slowly, he pressed down with his front paws and attempted to stand, but he wobbled and fell over sideways. The thinly crusted wounds that had formed a faint scab overnight broke open, and crimson blood poured into the dirt, but once more, he righted himself and pushed up on his legs. This time, he rose. He could hear

Achilles whimpering mightily behind him, and in the corner of his eyes, he could see the pale white of Delilah's dirty coat as she looked on, motionless.

When he rose to his feet, he looked once more to the forest, seeking a landmark to anchor his vision. He stared across the open field and fixed his eyes on the craggy bark of an old hemlock tree just at the edge of the forest. The tree seemed to waver and bend, and Goose struggled to focus his eyes, fighting to straighten the tree in his mind. His legs wobbled and his muscles ached, but he fought valiantly to remain upright.

As the sun rose high in the sky, the jagged rays of light streaked into the side of his vision, and the trunk of the tree seemed to glow in the warm light. He stared ahead, pushing through the sun's rays and focusing on the base of the tree. There, just behind the tree, in a patch of mountain shrubs dotted with wildflowers, a pair of narrow, amber eyes watched him. Goose blinked his eyes and focused, straining his vision into the forest, but when he did, they were gone.

He tottered to one side and then wobbled suddenly and fell, crashing hard into the ground. Across the yard, he could hear Zeus let out a single, sharp bark at the commotion.

All morning, as the sun baked the muddy ground, Goose lay in the dirt before his blue barrel.

THE DOG IN THE HOLLOW

Occasionally, he would shake his head limply to drive the horse flies away, but largely, he gave himself to the hollow and whatever awaited him.

At midday, the sound of the old screen door slapping against the house woke him, and he slowly lifted his head from the dirt. When he did, a sharp pain drove through his body, and he winced. He could hear chains clinking all around him as the dogs moved hungrily toward the source of the sound.

The Man's heavy footsteps pounded across the dirt. To Goose's right, Delilah jumped toward him. The chain pulled taut in midair, and she sprang backward, landing hard. She was back on her feet immediately, her sharp barks increasing in pitch as the Man moved closer to the yard carrying the bucket.

Only when the scent of the moldy kibble hit his nostrils did Goose realize the hunger that brewed in his belly. He reached his front paws out and crawled toward the man. As he crawled, he noticed for the first time the scabbed and bloody wounds that peppered his snout. Sickly brown-red streaks lined his face like dried, bloody streams. His vision had cleared somewhat, and he could see the Man approaching, his taut, wiry arms poking from the wide sleeves of a white t-shirt. The Man looked at Delilah dispassionately as she whined and whimpered for a bowl of rotten kibble. She jumped at him as he approached, and her paws clawed up and down the leg of his blue jeans. He twisted his knee hard into her, and she fell back once more and then sprang to her feet and thrust her hungry snout at the edge of the bucket as he poured her morsels into the bowl.

Then he turned and headed toward Goose, the bucket swinging in his right hand. Goose pressed his paws into the dirt, mustering the strength to rise to his feet. As the Man approached, he pushed his front end up and sat on his haunches, his body crooked and twisted in the dirt. His bones seemed to throb, and a tremendous torrent of pain raced down the length of his spine, yet he was hungry, and his mouth dropped to a friendly pant as the man approached. But then, he simply walked past, not even making eye contact with Goose.

"You didn't earn any food," the Man said sourly after he had passed.

Goose sat upright for a moment, unable to turn himself. His hungry eyes stared ahead, and Delilah turned on her chain to face him, her bowl rattling on the ground. When Goose heard the kibble hit Achilles' bowl behind him, he knew there would be none for him today, and he dropped to the ground in a huff and rested his chin on the ground. Delilah stared at him. Her crystal blue eyes shone brightly against her dingy white coat. She looked sympathetic to his plight.

After the Man fed the others, he stomped brusquely back into the house. The sun drew straight above the hollow and shone down on the dogs. Most of them retreated to their barrels, seeking shade. Occasionally, Goose mustered the strength to lift his head as his eyes searched aimlessly across the yard and the forest. In her barrel, he could see Rocket cowering from the world. It seemed she never slept, for whenever Goose looked in her direction, he could see the shimmer of her eyes, open and scanning the world beyond her barrel.

In the afternoon, a crisp wind blew through the trees and swept over the hollow. The ruffling of his fur brought a moment of solace for Goose as the gentle breeze soothed his open wounds and drove the horse flies away if only for a short while. As the day went on, he found the strength to rise to his feet, and several times, he stood as if testing the strength of his legs. His neck throbbed with a deep, sharp pain whenever he twisted his head, and the wounds on his snout felt like the quills of a porcupine, driven deep into his flesh. His front left leg was swollen into a bulbous mass that forced him to limp gingerly the scant few times he mustered the strength to take a few steps from his resting spot.

The entire day, he could sense that Queen was watching him, but he averted his gaze from her. He had enough to worry about now, and he kept his eyes toward Delilah and occasionally Rocket. Behind him, Achilles whimpered occasionally, and he knew his brother was watching with anticipation as he rose and attempted to walk around. Toward the end of the day, bored and hungry, he turned and looked across the yard at her.

Queen sat there at the end of her chain, resting comfortably on her haunches. She rested placidly, her calm demeanor in sharp contrast to the ghastly diagonal scar that stretched across her snout. Her chest was marred with streaks of dark red, but her eyes were clear, and her spirit was whole. She stared at Goose as he turned toward her, but this time felt different. He sensed no malice in the dog. She simply watched him as the dogs would watch the goshawks that arced and circled the yard — studying and admiring something foreign and unattainable.

Slowly, the sun fell over the hollow, and the rays faded beyond the dark silhouettes of the towering trees. The sky turned a dusky gray, and the droning chorus of katydids rose from the forest. Beyond the stand of mixed oaks, the lights in the house illuminated, and Goose could just hear the strange faint noise of the television pressing through the windowpanes.

Once more, he pressed his paws to the ground and rose to his feet, turning toward the blue barrel. As he took a step forward, a piercing pain shot down the length of his swollen leg. He instinctively shifted his weight to his right side, and his body buckled. He fell hard to his side, and as he did, he felt the tension on his collar release. He heard the chain rattle and fall to the dirt as he thudded into the dirt. All around him, he could hear the dogs stirring at the commotion.

Goose closed his eyes, and his mind sank into the pain, willing it to leave his body. He lay there for several minutes until the sharpness of a thousand nerves screaming in agony faded to a dull throbbing. Above him, the moon crept slowly into the sky, and the silvered rays stretched across the hollow, casting the dogs in a pale glow. Finally, after some time, Goose attempted to rise to his feet, seeking the meager safety of his blue barrel.

He rose slowly, tenderly pressing his left paw into the ground to brace himself. Lifting his back end, he raised himself to all fours and stood there, assessing his strength. As he did, a brief flash of metal shimmering in the moon's rays drew his attention, and he turned and looked down beside him. The dulled chain rested in the dirt, coiled like a dead serpent, and there, at the end, was the padlock. The clasp lay twisted wide open. He studied it for a moment, never having seen it like that. He only knew the lock when the Man brought it swiftly below his chin and clasped it tight to his collar. But now, it lay open, unfastened in the Man's haste and anger the night before.

Goose looked up to the blue barrel and then back to the lock. Gently, he stepped forward, waiting for the usual tension of the chain, but there was none. He stepped again, and a sharp pain shot up his leg, but once more, there was no tension. Nearby, Achilles whimpered at his brother. Goose turned and looked at him — in the darkness, he could see the anxiety etched on his face.

Goose took another step, and he was at the blue barrel. He turned and looked over his left shoulder, and still the chain rested there in the black shadows.

He was free.

Achilles whimpered again, and Goose looked at his brother, whose eyes shone brightly under the shimmering moon. His expression was one of unmistakable excitement as if he were the one who was free and could flee this place.

Once more, Achilles whimpered.

Go.

And without hesitation, Goose stepped forward with his right leg and began to stumble toward the wood line. Each step was excruciating as the pain shot straight up his shoulder and seemed to drive deep into his spine. His whole body trembled, yet he pushed forward, loping slowly off the rough dirt of the yard. His paws touched the tall grass that tickled his underbelly and made him forget the pain for a second until his left leg planted once more. When it did, he whimpered and stumbled forward. Behind him, Achilles barked a shrill cry.

Go!

At the sound, Goose pressed forward, and his vision began to cloud once more. The distant dark trees ahead began to waver and bend. A shroud of blackness started to draw over his eyes. He took one step more and then another, and the forest drew closer. He had never known pain like this before, and he longed to fall in the grass and let the darkness consume him, but he pressed on.

Behind him, he could hear Delilah barking and the rattling of chains. Soon, the sounds faded beyond the pulsing of his heart that echoed in his ears. Once more, he pressed off on his leg and lurched forward, nearly falling into the mountain shrubs at the edge of the clearing. As he reached the edge, the adrenaline coursed through him, and he could sense freedom. He pushed forward into the woods, fighting back the pain, and soon, the blackness of the forest consumed him. Unable to see, he limped forward as the ground began to slope upwards. The pain was almost unbearable, but he knew he must continue. He turned slightly to his left, moving up the slope diagonally, and began pressing his way through small shrubs and foliage.

His chest heaved, and he was panting heavily, exhausted. With one more step, he ran headfirst into a thicket. As the thorns raked across his sides, he staggered and fell, his chin skidding over the brambles. Once more, his eyes began to cloud, and the blackness drew to an impenetrable shroud. He reached out with his right paw and clawed into the ground, dragging himself forward. Then he reached with his left and, despite the pain, pulled his body across the ground. Inch by inch, he willed himself forward from the thicket. He was gasping for breath, and his mouth gaped open, sucking in air. His ribs ached each time he inhaled. Again, he reached out with his right paw and, once more, pulled himself forward, unable to see at all. Then, he reached out with his left and began to crawl, but the pain, like nothing he had ever felt before, was too much, and the darkness swallowed him.

CHAPTER 4

As dawn inched its way across the mountain, Goose awoke beneath the boughs of a hemlock tree. He could sense the presence of another nearby, and he felt the occasional gentle wisps of breath ruffle the fur atop the crown of his head. Fear welled within him, and his eyes flickered open as he instinctively rose to stand and then run. As he did, the pain rushed up his leg once more, and he winced and buckled. Beside him, he heard paws shuffle backward away from the commotion, and he turned his head to look.

There, in the shadows of the great forest, just feet away, the narrow amber eyes met his, and the two canines stood motionless on the slope of the mountain, awaiting the other's move. Goose studied the coyote who stood before him, searching his expression for signs of motive or ill intent. Yet, he found none.

In the shadows, the coyote's shaggy fur looked

drab and gray, but in the shafts of light that poked through the treetops, Goose could see hints of alabaster, beige, and soft tawny brown. His head was lowered, and his rear leg pressed forward slightly as if ready to run at any moment. He held his front right leg in the air, and it dangled there just inches above the ground.

Goose shook himself, shaking the brambles from his rear end. At the movement, the coyote backpedaled and seemed to angle awkwardly as he planted his paws to the ground and shuffled back a pace from Goose.

Around them, a cheery chorus of robins and the gentle lilting song of a hermit thrush cascaded through the forest. A soft wind whistled from the hollow below, rustling the mountain shrubs.

Unable to flee and sensing no threat from the coyote, Goose rested on his haunches. His mouth opened into a pant, and his eyes scanned the forest for any chance of escape. When he did, the coyote rested on his haunches as well, his body settling comfortably in a tight, upright sitting position. As he did, his right leg passed through the shafts of sun that angled through the forest canopy, and for the first time, Goose saw that he was missing his paw — a pale, knobby bone protruded where it should have been. The coyote pressed his other paw and the nub into the ground, giving him an unusually canted appearance. He looked upon Goose thoughtfully; his eyes were at once benevolent but intense.

He will come for you.

A shiver ran up Goose's spine as his mind flashed with violent memories from inside the trailer. He could smell the foul odor of the men, and he could taste the bitterness of his own blood as it trickled down his snout and rolled into his mouth. His bones seemed to throb at the memory of the Man dropping him hard on the dirt just outside his blue barrel.

The coyote could sense his fear. His eyes narrowed, and he seemed to study Goose, scanning the wounds on his neck and then settling on his swollen left leg.

Come.

Goose stared back at him, and the thought of trudging through the forest conjured pain in his leg. He winced at the mere idea.

The distance is short. You must hide.

Without anything further, the coyote rose from his haunches and began to move down the slope of the mountain, passing before Goose just a foot away with his back turned in a display of trust. Though missing a paw, the coyote moved nimbly, his feet seeming to glide across the forest floor. His limp was barely perceptible as he slowly trotted ahead with his head high and his tail low.

As he scaled higher up the slope at an angle, Goose watched him, confused at his predicament. He turned to his left and glanced down the slope through the trees. At the edge of his vision, he could just see the darkness of the forest lighten and give way to the hollow. As the morning breeze rustled through the treetops, he could smell the faint scent of the dogs below in the distance. His body was tired, his gums were dry as winter spruce bark, and his belly rumbled with a roaring hunger. Though his vision had cleared and the sharp stabbing that throbbed in his neck had subsided to a dull pain, he knew he would not make it far through these woods. Somehow, despite the horrors he had known there, the hollow below beckoned — the only home he had ever known.

Just then, the slapping metal of the screen door shot through the forest like a bullet. The trees seemed to shiver around him, and Goose hunkered low at the noise. To his right, he heard paws shuffling and turned — the coyote gazed down at him through the trees, his gray-beige coat blending seamlessly into the shadows. His expression was grave and urgent. Goose knew he must follow.

Stretching one paw in front of the other, he slowly pulled himself from the brambles and began to walk along the almost invisible footpath on which the coyote had traveled. The pain pulsed down his leg, and he felt light-headed from hunger, but he pressed onward. Step by step, they climbed higher through the forest up the gentle slope. With each lumbering stride, Goose steeled himself to the pain, learning the cadence of the nerves that fired into his brain and willing himself onward.

Below, he could hear the dogs barking, calling for their scant kibble. He knew the Man had come to feed them, and soon, he would know that he was gone. Through the forest, he could hear Delilah's high-pitched yelping. It pierced through the wall of trees and then, just as soon as it had come, carried away on the gentle wind. Occasionally, he heard Zeus's short, stoic barks.

As they climbed higher and higher, he heard Achilles yelping feverishly for something more than food.

Run, brother. Run.

Goose pressed onward, closing the distance to the coyote, who turned and looked at him. Goose couldn't help but notice how lean and angular he was, as if his whole body was made to knife through the forest, cutting through trees and leaping over the craggy rocks. The strange canine was unlike the others Goose had known.

The coyote sensed Goose's determination and picked up the pace. At times, it seemed his nub of a paw never touched the ground as he seemed to float over the surface, barely skimming the rocky soil and the low, leafy shrubs that covered the forest floor.

"Gooooooooose!!!!" came the shout from far below in the hollow. The Man called his name with a familiarity intended to summon him home, but his voice was unmistakably fierce and angry.

Goose stopped in his tracks and gazed down into the hollow.

You belong to the forest now.

Goose turned sharply back toward the slope, and the coyote was staring at him, his eyes seemed to glow with profound wisdom. Then the lean figure turned and continued up the slope, and Goose followed, beginning to limp heavily once more. Each time he stopped his cadence, the pain seemed to pool within him, and the next step became excruciating. He staggered slowly behind the coyote, who noticed his struggle and slowed his pace.

We are near.

Goose pressed onward, but his left leg buckled, and he staggered forward, almost falling before catching himself. His mind grew dizzy, and his vision began to cloud again. Then, he felt the gentle touch of the coyote as he dipped the crown of his head into Goose's cheek and nuzzled him. His soft fur felt rich and foreign, rousing Goose from the blackness that drew over him.

The coyote turned and trotted across the slope, and Goose followed as best as he could. Just when he felt he could go no further, the coyote stopped beside the base of a toppled spruce tree that had broken several feet up the trunk and fell toward the hollow, stretching the roots upward from the ground. The coyote dipped his nose into the blackness beneath the trunk and then turned and made sure Goose was watching him. Then, he tucked his belly to the forest floor and slithered into the blackness of the hole. The tan wisps of his tail vanished, and Goose stood there alone in the forest. Just as quickly, the coyote emerged, his pointy snout broaching the blackness, his legs clawing the forest floor to pull himself from the hole. He stood there looking at Goose, urging him to enter

Goose hesitated. The close confines of his blue barrel were one thing, but he was wary to crawl into the strange blackness beneath a fallen tree.

The coyote stared at him, his narrow eyes urging him to enter once more.

You must rest and hide.

Goose looked back at him. His body ached fiercely, and he longed to curl into a ball and let the darkness consume him. Hesitantly, he stepped forward into the hole. He could smell the damp soil and the scents of worms burrowing beneath the roots. He looked once more at the coyote, and then slowly, he lowered himself to his belly and pressed his nose into the blackness. In the dark, he could see a circular lair carved from the ground. The dark hole looked more inviting than Goose had anticipated, and inch by inch, he crawled forward.

Then, behind him, he heard the Man's voice frighteningly close.

"Goose!!" he bellowed.

Hurry.

Goose stretched forward with his paws and pulled himself deeper into the hole. He could feel his tail slip beneath the roots, and his rear legs dropped into the pitch-black lair.

"Goose!" came the shouts, much closer now.

Rest. I will return.

With that, Goose watched from below the forest floor as the coyote's legs darted off into the distance.

BLAMMM!

The sound of the gunshot thundered through the opening of the lair, and Goose's ears pounded as the noise echoed across the tiny chamber. His eyes drew wide open, and he curled tightly into a ball, pressing his body deep within the shadows.

Outside, he could hear footsteps approaching, and he could smell the wisps of gunpowder as they trickled through the tiny opening. Then, he could smell the Man's familiar, musky odor, and he knew that he was near.

On the other side of the tree, he could hear the slow, intentional rustling of bushes. He heard two more footsteps crunch closer across the rocks. Once more, the bushes rustled, and then he heard the noise of paws darting across the forest floor — one, two, three, one, two, three.

BLAMMM!!!

Again, the soil beneath the tree seemed to rumble. Goose felt the fat beetles digging deeper into the ground, fleeing the violent sounds.

"Didn't think you'd make it to mornin'. You've got more game than I gave you credit for!" shouted the Man, just outside the lair. "Show yourself just one more time!"

Goose tucked his nose deeper into his tail and tried to control his breathing. He closed his eyes and envisioned a sea of blackness engulfing him and silencing the noises and terror that lay just outside the hole.

Then, the Man's footsteps pounded across the forest floor and faded away. The forest was silent for a long time, and soon, the haunting chorus of the hermit thrush echoed through the trees, and Goose knew he was gone.

He lay there in the coyote's lair for the entire

day. Outside, he could see the light receding, claimed by the shadows, and the world outside grew a deep, inky black. Exhausted, Goose closed his eyes and fell into a deep, restful slumber.

He awoke in the morning, his eyes slowly opening. His jaws stretched wide in a deep yawn, and he blinked to clear the fog from his mind. Outside, he could see the pale shafts of morning light stretching through the forest. Considering his wounds, his body felt strong and rested, and the fog in his mind had cleared.

As he shook the last vestiges of slumber from his mind, his stomach rumbled, and his tongue pressed to the sides of his dry gums. He knew that, although he was stronger, he must eat and drink. He sniffed at the air. The scent of damp soil and the dung of insects filled his nostrils. But there was something else. He craned his neck toward the opening, sniffing into the morning air. Above him, the narrow face of the coyote peered down over the edge, his amber eyes backlit against the tall black trees that stretched into the morning sky. Goose looked back at him. The coyote sensed the strength in him and seemed pleased.

Follow. Water.

With that, the lean, gray-brown shape vanished from the opening, and Goose could hear his feet trotting slowly across the forest. Without hesitation,

THE DOG IN THE HOLLOW

Goose stretched his paws forward and pulled himself from the hole. His body ached, but the pain was dull and tolerable. The cool soil of the coyote's lair had soothed his tired muscles. He stretched his left paw forward and braced for the pain, but he found very little. He stepped forward on his right side and then again on his left, testing the leg. The pain was tolerable this morning.

To his left, a blur of tan fur moved as the coyote darted diagonally up the slope, higher and higher into the mountain forest. Goose ran after him in something of a hurried limp. The two canines pressed onward through the forest as the sun rose above them. After some time, the coyote stopped, and his ears perked and twisted forward, listening for the waters of the mountain stream. Goose could hear it too; the faint sound of moving water invigorated him, and he galloped after the coyote as they charged toward the source.

Soon, they reached a craggy rock outgrowth, and the coyote climbed up it nimbly, like a creature made to run on these rocks. Goose followed slowly, stepping gently across the strange rocks and pulling his tired body upward with some effort. At the top of the rock, the coyote dipped his head into the mountain shrubs, and Goose followed him. They emerged on the other side, and inches before them, the clear, bubbling waters of a shallow stream rushed down the slope of the mountain, crashing over small rocks and the long-dead branches of trees. The coyote turned and looked at Goose, clearly pleased at the dog's efforts.

Goose stepped forward and dipped his nose into the stream. The cool water splashed across his cheek and snout, and a life-giving chill ran down the length of his body. He lapped mightily with his tongue, sucking in the clean water. He drank until he could drink no more and his belly swelled with the fresh water. He sat back on his haunches, his buckskin coat damp with the stream's waters. For the first time in his life, he felt peace.

Together, they sat by the edge of the stream. The rushing water soothed Goose's mind, and he felt as if he could sit there for days. But before long, the pangs of hunger returned and, with them, the aching of his leg and the wounds on his neck.

The coyote seemed to sense the shift in Goose's mind. He rose to his feet and began trotting back through the shrubs. Goose followed, and they found themselves once more on an outcropping of craggy rock.

The coyote looked at him.

I will take you to a friend.

Without waiting for Goose's reply, he leapt from the rock to the forest floor and scaled higher and higher up the slope, zigzagging to avoid the steep inclines. Goose followed him, and throughout the rest of the day, they pressed on through the forest. In the afternoon, they reached a worn, narrow path. They walked along the path for quite some time, hugging the foliage near the edges to dart off into the forest should they see any signs of danger. After some distance, the coyote veered off the path and dipped into the forest. The trees seemed to thin, and the red spruce and hemlocks gave way to small stands of oaks and maples clustered among scattered foliage. The ground seemed to flatten. The two pressed on through the forest until the sun fell below the horizon and the silver wisps of moonlight sought refuge among the trees.

Goose grew more and more exhausted. He stepped forward, and his leg gave out from hunger and fatigue. He toppled to the ground, falling heavily into the leaves and thistles. The coyote stopped in his tracks and turned at the sound. He circled back and hovered over Goose.

Goose looked back at him. His eyes said he could not go any further.

The coyote simply stared blankly back at him.

Goose looked up at his amber eyes that seemed to quiver as his vision clouded. For a long while, Goose lay there on the ground. His legs ached, and his mind spun from fatigue and hunger. He opened his mouth and began to pant. The dried leaves before him crinkled and bent at his hot breath. He could feel the veins pulsing in his left leg, and once more, the sharp pains drove up his shoulder and into his mind. His eyes winced in pain.

I will not leave you.

There was a strange nobility about the coyote. Goose knew not why this strange creature helped him. Was he luring him into a trap? Running him until he was so weak that he could not defend himself?

No, there was something different about this one, something unlike the ones kept chained behind the old home or the ones that arrived in the night in cars at the end of taut leashes.

Goose knew that, if he was going to survive, he must trust the coyote. With every ounce of his spirit, he rose to his feet. He let out a howl of pain yet stumbled forward, gaining his balance.

The coyote studied him.

Good.

Then he turned and trotted into the woods, slowing his pace to allow Goose to keep up. The two of them pressed onward through the woods as night blotted out the sky above.

When they reached the edge of a tall stand of oaks and scrub brush, the coyote stopped, and Goose stumbled up beside him. His eyes focused into the darkness, and slowly, an unnatural, square, black shape became apparent in the distance. He squinted his eyes and focused again, and he could just make it out — the outline of a tiny, dark shack resting in a small clearing in the forest.

CHAPTER 5

L ooking out upon, the silhouette of the cabin through the tree line, Goose felt his stomach roil and turn. In his heart, he knew the structure meant humans; all he had ever known from them was cruelty. He was exhausted, but his mind urged him to flee. Turning toward the coyote, he wondered whether he had been lured here for some purpose.

But even if his broken body could have fled, it was too late. The coyote tilted his head skyward. The *yip yip* howl sent a shiver up Goose's spine and seemed to carry across the entire forest. On many a starry night, Goose had heard the haunting sound from the trees beyond the hollow. Whenever he did, he would huddle deeper into the blue barrel, pressing further into the darkness away from the frightening sounds far off in the black forest. Yet, at the same time, this song of lonesome solitude carried a sense of freedom that made Goose long for the hidden wonders of the woods. Now, he knew the source of the howl, and the last few days had taught him the travails of freedom.

When he finished howling, the coyote turned and angled his lean body toward the forest. As he did, he lowered his head toward Goose, and in the moonlight, his eyes glimmered majestically.

He is a friend.

Then, the coyote disappeared into the underbrush, and the sound of his racing footsteps carried deeper into the forest until the inky black night fell to a still silence. Goose sat there frozen. His heart raced, and he could feel the pulsing of the veins up and down his legs. He pressed down on his front left paw, testing his ability to flee.

As he did, the stillness vanished with the slow creaking of thick iron hinges, tired and weary, unlike the harsh slapping of the metal door at the old house in the hollow. From the silhouette of the shack, he could hear footsteps shuffling, and he sensed the presence of a man, though he could not see him through the darkness.

"Fenton?" called the soft, gravelly voice, whispering into the forest with quiet reverence.

Goose sat silently in the scrub brush, not daring to move. His eyes darted left and right, and subconsciously, he licked his lips. He felt trapped. He wouldn't get very far in the condition he was in, and even if he could run, he didn't know which way to go. The coyote had tricked him after all.

"Fenton?" rasped the voice, just barely above a whisper.

From the sound, Goose could tell the man was facing in his direction. He leaned forward on his legs, preparing to run. As he did, the thin, dry branches of the scrub brush crackled beneath his weight.

Just then, a blinding white light streaked from the entrance to the shack and lit up the forest all around him. He winced and closed his eyes, leaning backward from the oppressive glare.

Beyond the light, he could hear the man speaking indecipherably. Then he heard the slow thud of footsteps approaching him. He angled himself away from the light and opened his eyes, seeking a path to flee. The bright aura made him wince, and he struggled to make out the shapes of trees in the forest. Blindly, he stepped forward, and his leg throbbed, but he knew he must run. He took one more step, and then his legs buckled, and he fought to stay upright. The light beside him grew larger and larger as if a thousand moons would consume him whole.

Then, he felt a gentle touch on his shoulder, and he heard the man's voice just beside him.

"Shhhhhh....," said the man softly.

THE DOG IN THE HOLLOW

Goose felt his hand stroke slowly across his shoulder. The sensation was at once soothing but foreign. In his young life, he had never felt the kind stroke of a hand like this.

The man shone his bright light into the dirt, and the shadows crept over the forest once more. Goose stepped forward again slowly, although deep inside, his heart now told him to stay.

Again, the hand stroked across his side. "You're hurt," said the voice softly from somewhere in the blackness.

Goose stood motionless, unsure whether to run. He sensed the man lowering to crouch beside him, and he heard the crunch of his knees in the dried leaves. Then, the light flickered off, and the two sat alone in the blackness of the forest. Still, the man's hand gently stroked across his side and down his neck. Goose could feel the hand rubbing gently across his scabbed wounds, and for a second, it paused as and then continued, moving back to the smooth, short fur of his coat.

For several long minutes, the two sat in the darkness of the woods in an uneasy truce. Slowly and begrudgingly, the tension began to leave Goose's body, and his legs grew weary. Tentatively, he rested on his haunches, his eyes still staring ahead into the forest. Now that the glaring light had subsided, he could make out the dark silhouettes of the trees, and in his mind, he marked the path where he would run. But for now, he would stay.

"Did Fenton find you out in the woods?" asked the voice as he continued stroking Goose's side.

In the distance, Goose could hear the gentle trill of a Whippoorwill somewhere far in the forest. The bird's call was tranquil, and the movement of the man's hand flowed as if in cadence with the song. The path of flight he had marked soon faded from his mind. All around him, the shadowy trees no longer seemed like strange markers from a foreign place, but instead seemed to embrace him beneath their boughs. On his side, the man's hand was as soft as the welcome winds that blew across the hollow in a sweltering gaze.

Slowly, Goose stretched out his front paws, and his body began to slide until his full body rested upon the ground. As he did, he could sense the man leaning away to give him space. When he had settled atop the leaves, the man's hand returned and stroked the length of his back. He could feel the man's fingers following the rise and fall of his spine, and in the blackness, he could sense the man's heart was heavy.

For several minutes, Goose rested there with the man crouched beside him quietly. In the great distance through the forest, Goose could see the blackness lighten as the earliest rays of the sun kissed the dark sky. Then, he felt the man's hand gently slide beneath his stomach. For a moment, his body tensed, and his eyes searched the forest again for the path to escape. The man paused for a moment, and his patience calmed Goose. Then, he could hear the man rise from his knees. He felt his other hand slide under the other side, and the man embraced his whole body with hands on either side. Goose was tired, and the night was long, so he gave himself to the man.

"I promise I won't hurt you," he said then he lifted Goose from the ground with a grunt. The dog went limp, and his rear legs dangled heavily behind him. His eyes turned toward the man, and still, he saw only shadows in the waning hours of night. The man reached under his legs and tucked his hand beneath Goose's rear end and cradled him against his chest. Slowly, he stepped toward the old shack. Goose could hear him breathing heavily, and he could feel his spindly chest rising and falling.

Step by step, the man carried Goose across the short distance of the forest to the edge of the shack. As they approached, Goose could see the door gaping open, and a faint light glowed inside. The man stepped up from the forest floor to the tall entrance and twisted himself so he and Goose could pass through the narrow opening.

As they entered, Goose could smell the human

scents that hung heavy in the air. All he had ever known was the blue barrel and the old trailer; he had never set foot inside a real home. To him, the shack brimmed with the richest splendor. He could smell the scents of the man permeating the wooden walls of the place. His nose twitched, and his belly rumbled as he smelled the man's food. So many strange smells in this place, including the faint tinge of propane, the mildew of old wood, and the powdery fragrance of forest flowers. But beyond the smells, he could feel a darkness that hung over this place — solitary and melancholy.

The man stepped two paces into the tiny shack, and he was almost at the far wall. Gently, he bent over and rested Goose on the wooden floor, making sure his paws touched and his legs braced before releasing his grip around his waist. Then, he turned his body and reached for the door, pulling it closed. The click of the latch frightened Goose, and he jumped at the sound.

"I'm sorry, friend," said the man apologetically.

Goose lifted his eyes upward, and for the first time, the man was something more than a silhouette in the forest. His sharp, lean face was crowned with a flock of gray and white hair that seemed to sprout in every direction. In the dim yellow light of an electric lantern, Goose could see faint traces of dirt that highlighted his bony cheeks.

THE DOG IN THE HOLLOW

A long beard fanned out beneath his rigid nose; the beard was much whiter than the flock of hair atop his head. Despite his disheveled appearance, Goose could sense goodness about this ragged man.

He walked to the corner of the shack and tilted the plastic shade on a red camping lantern, allowing more light to filter off the walls. The lantern rested on a wide table, barren save for the weathered picture of a smiling, blonde-haired woman in a simple wooden frame. Beside the table was a drab, cast iron stove, and next to that, in the corner, was a small bed set on a rusted metal frame, the rumpled covers as dilapidated as the man.

Sensing no threat, Goose bent his hindquarters and rested on the floor, taking pressure off his tired body. As he did, he sensed for the first time the rough woven carpet that spanned the center of the floor. He had seen a carpet like this outside the front door of Virgil's old, beige house where he had been only once after another dog had gotten too close in the yard and bitten his leg.

The man stood before Goose, just inside the small shack, and looked down on him. As his eyes scanned up and down the dog's resting body, they narrowed with concern. Slowly, the man lowered himself to a knee. Goose could smell faint hints of the man's odor mixed with dried sweat. As he lowered himself, Goose could see that he wore a dingy, wrinkled t-shirt and a pair of loose, gray sweatpants, so weathered and worn that the knees had faded into a drab white.

The man stroked his hand down Goose's side, and he leaned forward, studying the scabbed wounds on his neck. His eyes tightened, and Goose could not tell if he was angry or worried; the man's emotions were difficult to read. Then he rubbed his hands over the rest of Goose's body — not the soothing gentle strokes, but ones that told Goose he was looking for something. Each time his hand rested on a scab, he stopped, and his fingers splayed through the short fur of Goose's coat, considering the wound. As he did, Goose lowered the front of his body and rested fully on the ground with a soft sigh. The man stroked the crown of his head as if reassuring him that it was safe to do so.

Slowly, the man reached out his hand, and in the dim light of the shack, he touched Goose's front left arm. Goose shot upright, and his lip curled, but then, the pain of the sudden movement stifled the snarl, and he let out a soft whimper and dropped heavily back to the ground.

"Sorry," said the man softly as his eyes studied Goose's leg.

Goose looked straight ahead to the barren wall beside the bed, watching the man from the corner of his eye, wary of any attempt to touch his arm.

THE DOG IN THE HOLLOW

The man did not try.

"I'm glad Fenton brought you."

And with that, the man rose to his feet and walked to the other end of the shack. Behind him, Goose could hear the soft creaking of hinges, and he heard the man digging through something. Goose turned his head to the right slightly and watched the man. There, at the far end of the old metal bed frame, just beside a worn wooden table, the man leaned over and dug into a weathered chest, lifting several blankets in all shades and colors, some dark, some brightly colored and quilted, and one full of stuffing. The man turned his back on Goose and began folding the blankets into neat squares. One by one, he stacked them in the far corner of the shack with the fluffy one on top, and then he leaned down and patted them with his hands. When he was finished, he turned over his shoulder and looked at Goose. In the dim shadows of the shack, their eyes connected. From the outside, they looked upon each other blankly and emotionless, but each knew that something brewed within the other.

When he was finished, the man turned and stepped carefully around Goose, walking to the far end of the shack. He reached beneath the table with the lantern and the picture of the woman and dragged an old camping cooler across the wooden planks that formed the floor. The noise didn't startle

Goose this time. He had been watching the man closely.

The man reached above the table to the long shelves that stretched the length of the shack just atop a pair of small windows. Goose heard him rattling around in the shadows, and when he finished, he brought down a lime green plastic bowl and set it gently on the ground next to Goose. Then, he opened the camping cooler, lifted a plastic jug of water, and filled the bowl halfway. Goose sniffed at the water and stretched his head gently toward the bowl, but he did not rise. He simply lay there in the shadows on the woven carpet and watched the man.

The man's hand returned to the tall shelves in the shadows, and Goose heard the rustling of a plastic bag. From the shelves, the man brought down the remnants of a loaf of bread and a jar of peanut butter. He twisted the jar, and the rich scent filled the small shack. Goose rose to his feet immediately, and his stomach grumbled. He took two steps forward and stood beside the man, lifting his injured leg off the ground and looking upward. The yellow light of the lantern sparkled against his dark eyes, and the man looked down at him sympathetically.

"I could tell you were hungry," he said, and beneath his scraggly beard, Goose could see the faint shape of a smile. He felt the heaviness lift from the man's heart for just a moment as he dug into the jar with a thick, flat knife and slathered it across the bread. When he was finished, he placed the two pieces together and turned to Goose, extending his hand.

Goose gnashed with his teeth hungrily at the sandwich, and the man startled backward, dropping it on the floor. Goose dipped his head and devoured it ravenously. He looked up and he could tell the man was nervous. Goose regretted being so hungry. He blinked his eyes at the man to show him he was sorry, and then he rested on his haunches to show him even more.

He could feel the nerves leaving the man, and slowly, he turned once more and dipped the flat knife into the jar and slathered the peanut butter on the bread and placed the pieces together. Goose rose from his feet as the man turned, but then he rested on his haunches, and his tail began to sweep slowly across the floor, left and right. The man seemed pleased with him as he held the sandwich high. Goose opened his mouth and began to pant. Then, the man cautiously dropped the sandwich on the ground. Goose looked at it once and then at the man and then lowered his head and, in a great chomp, clenched the sandwich and swallowed it almost whole.

"That should hold you over for now," said the man as he looked down, studying Goose. Then he turned and walked across the shack, stooping to grab the plastic bowl that he carried to the corner near the bed of blankets on the floor. He stood there looking back at Goose, and then he bent over and patted the bed.

"This is for you," he said and then paused. Goose could see his eyes studying him from the shadows. "Much nicer than where you came from, I'm sure."

Goose sat there in the center of the shack, unsure of himself. He glanced back over his shoulder to the dark shelves where the man had returned the jar and then back to the other side of the shack at the man. The man patted the blankets again, and Goose slowly walked forward across the shack and stood before the blankets, unsure. The man placed his hand behind Goose's front leg and pressed lightly. Goose stepped forward onto the stack of blankets, and he could feel the strange softness. Unbidden, he took another step until his whole body was on the blankets. He spun so his rear end faced the corner of the shack and then dropped his body heavily until he was curled beside the man. He lifted his nose and noticed the green plastic bowl and then, without rising, stretched his neck and extended his tongue, lapping at the cool water until he was full.

Then, the man rose to his feet and looked down at the dog. In the shadows, Goose could sense he was smiling. "I'll see you in the morning, friend," said the man, and he shuffled a few steps across the wooden floor to the red camping lantern, flicked the switch, then climbed into the old bed. The shack fell to darkness save for the slivers of moonlight that trickled through the forest canopy. Outside the window, the Whippoorwill trilled its haunting song, and the man and the dog fell to sleep.

CHAPTER 6

Goose woke to the sounds of the man entering the shack. As the door opened, the light of early dawn pressed upon him. The man stood there in the doorway, looking to the corner. Lying on his side, Goose stretched his legs straight before himself and pushed away the remnants of a deep slumber. Never had he slept the whole night without waking from terrible sounds outside his blue barrel or the hunger that rumbled his stomach. His body felt strange and detached for a moment as it adjusted to the sensation of true rest. He lifted his head and looked at the man and then, thinking better of it, lowered his head back to the soft blankets and closed his eyes. He heard the man chuckle softly and then step into the shack, the door propped open behind him.

From beyond the doorway, a gentle breeze blew into the shack and rustled the short furs of Goose's coat. If his bladder wasn't pressing urgently on his insides, he could sleep there forever. The open door of the shack seemed to call him to the forest, and so he rose slowly on his feet, and the man turned to watch him. He arched his back upward and leaned forward, stretching his legs. Already, his left leg felt better, although the deep, dull ache was undeniable.

"Come on," said the man, as he stepped in front of Goose and down to the forest floor just outside the cabin. Goose followed him, shambling slowly along on stiff legs and hesitating at the doorway as he lowered his front end carefully and stepped to the ground.

The air outside was warm, but Goose felt greeted with a freshness he had never felt below in the hollow. He looked around the forest and studied the towering trunks of the spruces crowded at their bases with shrub brush. He sniffed at the air, lifting his snout, and thought he smelled a familiar scent. He remembered the coyote now as his mind began to replay the night before. As he stood there looking out into the forest, the long journey came back to him, and his body seemed to ache from the memories. He remembered the smell of the soil beneath the fallen tree, the sounds of the beetles and insects burrowing into the ground, the terrifying thunder of the gunshots, and the long journey up the mountain to this place. He looked around the forest for the coyote, but he could not find him. Only his scent from the night before lingered faintly in the shrubs.

"Go on," said the man gently, waving his hand toward the forest.

Goose looked at him and, without further prodding, took several long steps to the edge of the clearing and raised his leg, urinating for almost a minute. His eyes closed in bliss as the pressure from his bladder relinquished its grip.

When he was finished, he turned and looked back toward the man and the shack. The man had sat down on a squat, weathered tree stump several feet beyond the front door of the ramshackle structure. He sat there hunched over with his elbows on his knees watching Goose. Goose looked back at him and studied him in the white light that seeped into the small clearing from beyond the towering trees. The man's face was lean and gaunt and looked back at Goose dispassionately. Goose felt somewhat uneasy at his inability to read the man. Back in the hollow, Virgil's expression was always one of scorn and contempt, and Goose knew what to expect. This man was far more complex. He had been kind to Goose and never bothered him as he slept on the tall stack of blankets in the corner of the shack. But now as he sat there on the tree stump, Goose could not sense his emotions.

THE DOG IN THE HOLLOW

As if the man knew what Goose was feeling, he lifted his arm from the worn knee of his blue jeans and motioned for Goose. "Come," was all he said. His eyes seemed to narrow, and his blue eyes sparkled behind his worn, tired face.

Goose stood there at the edge of the forest and looked back at the man. Above him, the needles of the tall spruce trees rustled in a soft breeze, and he could hear the sounds of squirrels traipsing through the forest. But he did not go to the man just yet.

His eyes softened as he could sense Goose's hesitation. "My name is Clarence," he said softly. "What's yours?" His lips creased upward beneath his shaggy beard. Then he looked down at the ground, his mouth still formed in a gentle smile.

Goose rested back on his haunches at the edge of the forest. He was not ready to come. But he was not ready to go.

"I don't get too many visitors in these parts," said Clarence, looking down at the forest floor before the stump. He began to rub his hands together, picking at the dirt on his palms with his thumbs. "Just old Fenton whenever he feels like coming around."

Clarence looked up at Goose and studied him closely. His eyes searched across the dog's body, studying the scars and tick marks where Rebel's teeth had clipped his fur from his flesh.

"I bet you've got some tales to tell." He paused for a moment, and then his eyes raised and he looked off into the forest over Goose's head. "I'll listen when you're ready." He rose from the stump and brushed the front of his dark t-shirt with his hand as if tidying himself then turned and walked back into the cabin. His shape disappeared into the shadows past the threshold, and Goose sat alone at the edge of the forest.

For a long time, Goose sat there, waiting for the man to return, but he never did. All around him, the creatures of the mountain stirred to life. Chipmunks darted through the underbrush, dragonflies circled the patches of wildflowers, and a northern flicker drummed away at the spruce tree high above.

Finally, Goose rose to his feet and looked around the clearing. To the left of the cabin, a dusty green plastic water container hung by a thick cord from the branch of an oak tree, spinning in slow circles with the morning breeze. In the distance behind the shack, Goose could see the rough stones of a fire pit and the remnants of broken, charred logs stacked neatly upon one another. Yet, aside from these scant human markings, he saw only the forest.

Slowly, he followed the fading trail of Fenton's scents to the shrub brush from the night before as if he might discover some secret there. He lifted his nose and sniffed all along the edges of the leaves, but he knew the coyote was long gone and there were no secrets here.

He turned and looked at the cabin and paused for a moment. The door was open, inviting him in, but he could not see Clarence, and he heard no noises. Finally, he gingerly walked toward the cabin, his eyes scanning the doorway, alert and ready to flee as quickly as his sore leg would let him. Though he limped slightly, the pain had subsided greatly with the night's rest, and he felt refreshed and alive.

When he reached the door, he lifted his nose and sniffed for Clarence's scent. He was just inside the door. Slowly, Goose poked his nose inside. Shafts of morning light slanted through the windows on the east side of the cabin, illuminating a patch across the floor where the woven carpet lay. There, in the corner to the right of the door, Clarence sat in a wooden chair leaning over a small oak desk pressed into the corner of the shack. Goose could see the pen in his right hand moving across a piece of paper as his left-hand held open an old worn book, illuminated by the light of a small lantern. He sensed Goose and turned slowly to look over his shoulder.

His face did not smile, but Goose could feel the

warmth within him.

"Are you going to join me?" he said. Then he turned away from Goose and returned to his writing, his eyes shifting back and forth between the page and the book. Goose stood there at the edge of the shack for several long moments and watched him. Then, he lifted his paws and stepped into the shack. As his nails clicked on the hardwood, Clarence stopped writing for a moment, and his head rose slightly, but he did not turn. Goose brought his rear legs into the cabin and walked slowly across the floor to the corner where his blankets lay, stepped on them, and then curled himself into a ball. He could feel Clarence smile as he continued writing.

For much of the day, Goose rested there in the blankets while Clarence sat at his desk, reading books and writing words with his pen. Goose did not know what he was writing, but he could feel that the task was natural to Clarence and could sense the fullness of his heart as he sat there at the old desk.

In the afternoon, Clarence rose and stretched his tall frame toward the ceiling. Goose could hear the creaking of his joints and the gentle popping of his back. Clarence rolled his head from left to right, releasing the kinks from his neck, and then he looked down at Goose, who returned his gaze.

THE DOG IN THE HOLLOW

"We should clean you up and take a look at those wounds," he said, his tone carrying a hint of worry. "After that, we'll have some lunch." Then he reached up high on one of the shelves that lined the cabin and retrieved a small metal box and a dull white towel. He turned and stepped outside the shack and into the light of day. Goose rose to follow him and then paused for a moment. Clarence stepped away into the clearing, and when Goose could no longer see him, he walked across the floor and lowered himself from the shack.

Near the tree with the water tank, the man rested the metal box on the ground and opened it. Inside, Goose could see white paper packages and metal tubes. Curious, he walked over to Clarence and sniffed in the box. Scents of menthol and chemicals filled his nostril, and he stepped away, disappointed that it was not food.

"We're going to have to get you wet, buddy," said Clarence, looking down at Goose. He reached up to the water container and turned the spigot, and a clear, cool stream of water poured to the ground, puddling in the bare dirt of the clearing.

Clarence reached out gently for Goose's collar. Goose leaned back on his paws, away from the water, but Clarence slipped his fingers under the collar and pulled him forward beneath the water.

"I know you don't like it, buddy." Carefully,

Clarence reached beneath Goose's chin, his fingers searching for the buckle on his thick, leather collar. When he found it, he pulled and tugged on the collar, and Goose could feel it constrict around his muscular throat as Clarence fought to free the buckle. Finally, Goose felt the pressure release, and he could feel the fresh air kiss the matted fur around his neck.

Clarence pulled the collar from around his neck and held it up in the air, inspecting it. His eyes squinted as he peered at the old metal plate studded to the leather collar. With his finger, he brushed away the dust, then he lifted the collar and held it beneath the flowing water and rubbed it once more with his finger. Finally, he could read the word etched into the metal plate.

GOOSE

Clarence looked at the collar for a moment and then down at Goose, and his eyes studied him without emotion. Then, he reached out his hand and tossed the collar into the clearing and returned to his work.

Slowly, Clarence rubbed the cool water into Goose's coat, his fingers working the moisture deep into his thin fur, rubbing away the dirt and filth from around his wounds. Clarence rested on his knees and pressed Goose into his chest, holding him tight as the water poured down upon the dog.

THE DOG IN THE HOLLOW

Silently, he rinsed the wounds, his hand rubbing along the crusted edges, sensing the scope of his injuries. When he was done, he reached up and turned the spigot, and the cascade of water stopped.

Then, Clarence took the old white towel and dried Goose, using his fingers to separate the fur around his wounds and lowering his head to look closely. Occasionally, Goose saw him frown as he looked at the wounds. Goose rested against his chest and gave himself to the man.

When he finished, Clarence reached into the box and retrieved one of the metal tubes. He opened it, and Goose could smell the strong medicinal scent, and it made him turn his head away. Clarence took heaping gobs of the clear gel and swathed it over the open wounds, rubbing it around the edges. Goose could feel the cold tingle when the gentle breeze hit the strange gel.

Then, Clarence released Goose and rose to his feet. "You're pretty beat up, buddy," he said and shook his head. "I wish I had something more to give you, but I think that will help." He leaned over and picked up the paper wrappers and cylinders from the metal box, placed them back inside, and closed the lid.

He looked down at Goose again. "I don't think your leg is broken the way you're walking on it." He turned and headed back into the shack. "But we'll keep an eye on it," he said over his shoulder and disappeared again into the doorway.

Afterward, Clarence slathered more peanut butter on the bread and placed it gently on the floor for Goose. He scoffed up the sandwiches and drank cool water from the green bowl.

"I suppose you need some real food if you're going to stay for a while," said the man, as he returned the saggy plastic bread bag to the shelf.

When the moon rose over the forest, Goose returned to the corner of the shack and curled himself into his blankets. For a long time, Clarence sat there at the desk, reading his books in the lantern light, until finally, he wiped his fingers against his eyelids wearily and rose. He stood from his chair and glanced down at Goose, resting nearby in the corner.

"Goodnight, buddy," he said. Then he pulled the door to the shack closed, turned off the light, and crawled into the bed.

CHAPTER 7

For three days, Goose remained at the shack. He spent most of his days resting on the pile of blankets which Clarence occasionally lifted and shook, releasing the rumples and fluffing them for his new roommate. Each morning, Goose followed Clarence out to the clearing, and the two stretched their tired joints and greeted the morning sun as it rose over the mountain. Clarence would walk to the dangling water container and wet a crooked blue toothbrush and brush his teeth, occasionally dampening his hair and body with a towel. While this ritual was underway, Goose relieved himself in the woods and explored the nearby forest, never straying far from the shack. His leg felt stronger with each passing day. Although the throbbing pain occasionally returned if he walked too far or stepped awkwardly, he mostly felt comfortable placing the full weight of his body on the leg, and the swelling had largely subsided.

The scabs on his neck and forearms were thick and dark now, and a few had started to rise at the edges and fall away, although the deeper punctures still occasionally oozed and bled.

For most of each day, Clarence would sit with his nose in a book on the old stump or rest in a worn green hammock strung from a pair of young spruces near the fire pit. Goose would always rest on the ground nearby, and he noticed that Clarence regularly lifted his gaze from the book to make sure he was still nearby.

Clarence still hadn't found any suitable food for Goose, and he seemed embarrassed when he filled the dog's plastic bowl with a sad mismatched casserole of leftovers, including cooked vegetables, scraps of bread, and bits of dried cereal. Goose never minded, and he ate hungrily, usually pleading with his eyes for more. On the third day, Clarence scraped at the last remnants of the peanut butter and wiped it in thin streaks on a slice of bread. Goose waited patiently now; that first day in the cabin when he snapped at the bread and frightened Clarence was a distant memory.

Clarence spoke few words to Goose, mostly in the morning when he led him out into the soft white of dawn and at night when he closed the door of the shack and shuffled off to the old bed in the corner. Occasionally, Clarence would ask a question. Goose could tell from the inflection in his voice, but he never knew what Clarence said, and he knew that an answer was not really expected. So, they carried on just the same.

On the fourth day, Goose stepped to the edge of the forest and relieved himself. When he finished, he stared out through the rigid trunks and narrowed his eyes, stretching his vision deeper and deeper through the trees. Beneath the warmth of the sun's rays, he envisioned the hollow and realized it was the first time in four days he had thought deeply of the place. Until now, his mind had been occupied with his mending body and the good fortune of his newfound situation. But now, with his belly full and having settled comfortably into a routine, his mind raced with thoughts of the other dogs he had left behind.

As he stared through the gaps between the shadowy spruces and gazed across the scattered beds of wildflowers, Achilles' barking echoed in his ears. In his mind, he could see himself hobbling from the yard and staggering in the forest. He knew that, somewhere down there beyond the endless forest, the others languished at the end of their chains. Through the matchstick trees that were barely visible in the far distance, he could almost see Queen's deep, onyx eyes staring at him. He looked to his left, where Rocket would have been, and in the shadows of the forest canopy, he could envision her fearful eyes, glimmering in the back of her blue barrel.

His heart sank at the thought of the hollow, and suddenly, the comfort and tranquility of this mountain clearing weighed on him heavily. He whimpered out into the forest as if, somehow, the winds that drifted down from the mountain would carry his voice to the hollow below and the others would know that he had not left them. But he knew they would never hear him from this place.

He must return.

Goose turned and trotted back to the shack, his legs feeling strong and sturdy. Inside the shack, Clarence sat inside at his desk with his head down and his eyes scanning the pages of an old, worn book. Goose barked, and the sudden, shrill noise startled Clarence, and he dropped the book and turned and looked at him, his eyes wide and perplexed. Goose barked again, a single loud noise that in any language could mean only, "Come."

Clarence leaned forward and peered his head out the open door to the shack and scanned the forest, looking for anything amiss. "What is it?" he asked with a hint of concern on his face.

Goose barked again, his eyes never leaving Clarence.

"Is it Fenton?" Clarence rose from his chair and

stepped out into the clearing, running his long fingers through his tousled hair. His blue eyes narrowed, and he scanned the forest. Seeing nothing, he looked down at Goose, who had moved out near the edge of the clearing and stood looking back at him. Then, Goose started into the forest, walking a short distance into the woods and beginning to head down the slope. Once more, he turned around and looked at Clarence, who stood there anxiously tugging at the front of his worn t-shirt.

Goose barked once more. Then he turned and headed further down the slope.

"Goose!" called Clarence, a hint of panic in his voice.

Behind him, Goose could hear Clarence's feet pounding away from him, and he heard him step up into the shack. Then, he heard the noise of something being dragged across the wooden floor. After a moment, Clarence stepped from the shack and pulled the door shut behind him. Slung over his shoulder with a tattered strap was an old, black-barreled rifle with a weathered wooden stock.

Clarence hurried to the edge of the clearing and looked down the slope, catching sight of the dog. Goose could sense his relief. Then, Goose started down the slope, and Clarence hurried along behind him, his worn boots crunching on the pine needles and fallen leaves.

For several hours, Goose pressed down the slope, heading toward the hollow. He had very little recollection of the path that Fenton had led him, so he followed his senses in the direction he felt pulled. He worried that he was not headed the right way, that he would get them both lost deep in the woods, and that Clarence would be upset with him and would leave him in the woods while he found his way back to the shack. But despite the worries, he pressed onward. The hollow summoned him.

As he picked his way down the slope, Clarence hurried along to keep up. While Goose's leg began to throb, the comfort of knowing that the bone was not broken energized him, and soon, the pain faded to a dull, numb sensation.

As he pressed his paws atop a fallen log and leapt over, landing roughly in a patch of fallen leaves, he heard Clarence call behind him.

"Goose," he said, gasping and out of breath.

Goose turned and could just see the top of Clarence's shaggy gray-white hair in the distance, beyond the fallen log. Clarence took several steps forward and then sat unceremoniously on the log, hunching over and breathing heavily with his elbows on his knees.

"We need to rest for a minute," he said, turning

his head until his blue eyes met Goose's.

Goose circled and walked back to the log, pressing his snout into Clarence's elbow, rousing him to continue. Clarence reached out with his right hand and stroked clumsily up and down Goose's neck as he panted heavily. Above them, the rays of the sun began to recede from the forest canopy as it started its slow, downward descent.

"Where are we going, anyway?" he said, lifting his head and scanning down the slope into the forest. "There's nothing out this way."

Goose rested on his haunches; it was evident that Clarence needed to rest for a moment. Goose turned his head and looked down the slope, his eyes searching the forest. All around, the sound of woodland creatures scurrying along the forest canopy and the drumming of woodpeckers filled the forest. He stared down the slope, focusing into the distance. His ears perked, and he strained his senses further and further through the trees. For a brief second, the tiny paws on the leaves stopped, and the beak of the woodpecker was still. In that moment, Goose could hear the almost imperceptible sound of barking far in the distance.

At the noise, he turned and sprinted down the slope, galloping over the shrub brushes, his legs pumping like pistons. Behind him, Clarence rose, startled, and swept his legs over the log, scurrying down the hill after Goose.

"Goose!" called Clarence, his voice growing faint in the distance.

Goose pressed his legs into the ground and skidded to a halt in the leaves. His ears perked, and he controlled his breathing and listened into the distance. Once more, he heard the faint sound of a bark, louder this time. He started forward again.

"Goose!" came Clarence's voice behind him, louder now and beginning to sound agitated for the first time. Goose stopped at the emotion and turned as Clarence came stumbling down the slope behind him, gasping for breath.

"You're going to run off into these woods, and I'm not going to be able to find you —" he huffed in erratic, ragged breaths, — "and whatever it is that you want to show me, I'm not going to see." He bent over, pressing his hands to his knees. The rifle slipped from his shoulder and swung like a pendulum.

And so, the man and the dog continued slowly down the slope together, Goose leading the way patiently and Clarence following him. Goose could feel that Clarence much preferred this pace, and though he longed to sprint ahead, he knew they must stay together.

As the sun dipped below the horizon and the tall spruce trunks rose into the chalky sky, Goose could sense the woods before him beginning to thin. On the faint breeze that swept up the slope, his nostrils caught the unmistakable scent of the other dogs not far below in the hollow. He eased his slow trot and began taking long, methodical steps through the foliage, carefully placing his paws to avoid the crunching of leaves. Behind him, Clarence noticed the shift in his demeanor and could now hear the distant sounds of dogs barking. Instinctively, he crouched lower and began walking on the balls of his feet, careful to avoid fallen branches and foliage that may snap and sound beneath his feet.

For several hundred yards, the two proceeded down the slope in this manner. The sounds of barking grew louder and louder with each step. Soon, the barking shifted from indecipherable noise until Goose could make out the individual voices. Nearest, he could hear Achilles, barking balefully into the forest, his voice tired and bored. Further away, he could hear Zeus returning Achilles's occasional barks with a challenge of his own, and he could hear the distant clinking of iron links that undoubtedly signaled him pulling at his chain.

The man and dog crept along until they came to the edge of the forest, where the spruce mixed with stands of oak and elm and the scrub brush grew high at the lip of the clearing. Above the hollow, the distant crescent of the impatient moon twinkled in the folds of the dusty sky, and a dying halo of light crested above the forest — the last act of the setting sun.

Goose pushed his nose into the shrub brush, and his eyes scanned the clearing. Clarence kneeled just behind him over his right shoulder. As expected, Zeus stood at the end of his chain, which was pulled taut as he leaned toward Achilles, who rested on his haunches in the dirt across the yard, occasionally barking in boredom. From the distance, Goose could not see into Rocket's barrel, but he had no doubt the dog was there, huddled far from the world. Beside Achilles, Delilah rested in the dirt, her nose down between her paws, staring off across the yard. On the other side of Achilles, Storm lay on her side, her belly exposed to the forest, and beside her, Queen sat like a statue, her black coat glistening in the last rays of the sun as she stared off into the mountain.

Goose looked toward his blue barrel that sat just as it had before. Beside it, he could just make out the iron axle driven deep into the ground, but it was barren of any chain. The Man must have taken it away once he discovered Goose had escaped.

Goose heard Clarence whisper over his shoulder. "So this is where you came from?" His voice was low and grave.

THE DOG IN THE HOLLOW

For a long while, the two sat in the shrubs staring out into the yard. Deep inside, Goose longed to run into the clearing and announce himself to the others, let them know he had not left them, but he knew it would do no good. He turned over his shoulder and looked at Clarence, his eyes asking the man to do something. Clarence looked back at him, but Goose could tell that he was unsure and afraid.

As night fell over the hollow, Goose jolted upright at the sound of the screen door slapping against the wooden side of the old house. He turned to his left and could see the beam of a flashlight dancing across the rough ridges of the old logging road. Then, he could hear the familiar footsteps of the Man pounding across the yard, and he heard the rattling of kibble in the plastic bucket.

The Man walked to the edge of the yard, and Delilah rose on her legs to greet him, jumping hungrily at the bucket. He kneed her away, and she spun backward, landing on her feet and charging back at him. He poured the bucket, and Goose heard the familiar sound of kibble rattling against the metal bowl but, this time, much scarcer than normal. Delilah dipped her head greedily into the bowl, and Goose could hear her lapping at pieces of kibble that rattled around the bowl and eluded her hungry jaws. Then, the darkness exploded with a snap-bang and the flash of a pistol's muzzle. Delilah's body went suddenly limp, and she sagged and fell heavily forward, her snout causing the metal bowl to flip upward and spin to the ground where it rolled on its edge and came to rest in the dirt.

In the still summer air, Goose could hear the malignancy in the Man's voice. "You ain't worth my food if you won't fight," he said as he prodded her limp body with his boot to make sure she was dead.

CHAPTER 8

For nearly an hour, they lay there in the bushes, man and dog panting heavily against the warm night air. Horse flies and mosquitoes buzzed around, drawn to the sweet scent of perspiration. Incessantly, Clarence scratched at the base of his neck and the crooks of his arms with his face twisted in a mask of consternation. Beside him, Goose rested on his haunches, his jaw slung open, and his great pink tongue splayed outward below his eyes, wide and afraid, staring ahead through the sweet ferns and scrub oaks into the hollow before them.

"Let's go," whispered Clarence, his voice set with determination. The leaves rustled softly as he gingerly rose to a crouch.

Goose only looked ahead, not responding.

Clarence reached out and stroked his hand down Goose's sweat-slicked fur. The touch roused Goose from his stupor, and he turned slightly toward Clarence. In the moonlight at the edge of the hollow, their eyes met.

In the pale whites staring back at him beneath the shaggy hair that bristled against the silvery, starlit backdrop, Goose could see within the man. He looked frightened, but there was something more, some deep reckoning brewing within his soul.

Goose rose to his feet and slowly turned from the hollow. In the distance, he heard the clinking of a chain pulling taut, and he knew that Queen had risen to her feet and was scanning the woods. Although she stood invisible far across the hollow with her jet-black coat shrouded in the inky night, Goose knew her eyes were upon him. A shiver ran up his spine, and he started forward as Clarence crept slowly up the edge of the mountain.

For several long hours, they walked through the woods in silence. Clarence said nothing, only occasionally turning around to make sure Goose was following without too much difficulty. Though his leg ached with each step they climbed, he felt a sense of purpose as he followed Clarence back to the cabin.

As they neared the crest, Goose could see the first tendrils of the morning sun stretching out over the jagged trees. Inch by inch, the forest slowly began to glimmer as the shafts of light lanced down to the leafy floor.

Clarence trudged slowly across the worn dirt to the cabin door. His legs seemed to wobble, and Goose sensed it was more fear than fatigue. As Clarence reached the door, he slipped the rifle off his shoulder, and it dropped swiftly until he caught the strap and let it dangle by his side. He reached for the door and pushed it open, stepping up into the cabin and disappearing into the darkness. Goose walked slowly behind him, his eyes surveying the surrounding forest anxiously. When he was sure the woods were quiet, he hopped up and slipped into the darkened structure behind Clarence.

Clarence lay there on the bed, his arms splayed outward beside him and his feet dangling unceremoniously over the edge. Goose stood there looking at him in silence. He watched Clarence's chest heave up and down in deep, steady breaths. In the close confines of the cabin, Goose could sense him; his emotions hung over the tiny structure like a dark, unsettled cloud. Goose could feel the conflict within the man, a strange sense of duty muted by a nervous apprehension as if some ill foreboding stifled his purpose.

On stiff, throbbing legs, Goose ambled to the corner toward the pile of blankets. He stepped forward with his front legs onto the soft fabric, circled in the corner and then unceremoniously lowered his shoulder and flopped to the bed exhausted.

The humid, still air of the cabin hung over him like a heavy fog. The shrill chirping of cicadas echoed outside the open door but seemed repelled from entering by the dead silence that lingered within. On the bed, Clarence's chest rose and fell more and more slowly as he regained his breath.

For a long time, the two of them lay in silence in the cabin alone with their thoughts. Goose's legs throbbed, and the pads of his paws were tender. Before him, the green bowl sat full of lukewarm water, but he hadn't the strength to stretch his neck mere inches to reach it. His eyes, half-closed, stared ahead into the black wall of the cabin. Deep inside his mind, thoughts churned in ill-formed visions, veiled behind a dark curtain of exhaustion. He fought to keep his eyes open, hoping Clarence would rise from the bed and break the dreadful silence that consumed the cabin. But soon, he could no longer fight the weariness that drew over him and closed his eyes to a deep slumber.

Goose woke at the soft vibration of Clarence's foot landing on the shack's wooden floor. As he opened his eyes and lifted his head, golden rays arced into the cabin through the open door, alighting a square patch on the dingy floor.

THE DOG IN THE HOLLOW

Clarence stood there just past the doorway and, at the movement, turned to look at Goose.

Goose studied Clarence's shadowed face, seeking to make sense of the man's emotions. Clarence looked back at him, and his expression was blank, but Goose knew there was life behind his features. Reaching out with his senses, Goose pressed deeper into Clarence, pushing behind the blank slate exterior and reaching out to touch his spirit. Then, he could feel it—a deep, churning storm brewing just below the surface, an unpleasant concoction of determination mixed with a deep apprehension of things to come. The two emotions pressed against each other, and Goose could sense a battle raging within the man, though he stood there stone-faced. When he looked at Goose, his eyes seemed to look through him, as if searching through visions and memories buried deep within his mind.

Goose lay there with his head on his paws and lowered his gaze, looking away from Clarence timidly; the storm raging inside the man frightened him. After a moment, Clarence blinked his eyes, and the bland exterior slowly started to fade as life returned to him. His eyes cleared, and now Goose could feel him genuinely looking at him and seeing him, not through him.

"Good morning, Goose," he said as if trying to

quell the discomforting atmosphere of the shack. Goose rolled his eyes upward and looked back at him but did not move.

Clarence stepped forward across the cabin, and an old plank creaked, breaking the silence. Slowly, he bent down and crouched to one knee before Goose. He reached out his thin, weathered hand and stroked it across the crown of Goose's head. Goose closed his eyes, bracing for the touch, and then he felt the kindness glide across the crown of his skull. Goose dipped his head and sank into the stack of blankets as Clarence stood there stroking him for a long time.

For much of the day, the two remained in the shack, a thoughtful silence resting over them. In the morning, Goose lapped up three bowls of water, his jaws dripping puddles on the shack floor. In silence, the two had eaten scraps of food and then napped again as the sun rose to its apex in the sky outside.

In the afternoon, Clarence stepped out of the cabin and sat on the old weathered stump, hunched over with his elbows against his knees, staring at the ground. Shortly thereafter, Goose rose from his bed and followed him, stepping silently down from the cabin and walking gingerly toward Clarence. As he drew close, he touched the fur of his side against Clarence's elbow, a gentle signal that he was here. Clarence didn't move, but Goose could feel his spirit rise.

Goose circled in front of him and dropped to the ground with a soft grunt and a gentle puff of dust. Clarence sat there motionless on the stump, and Goose could feel the clouds stirring within him again.

"What are we going to do?" Clarence said, looking up to the forest, his words soft and barely audible. "What are we going to do?" he said again, drawing out the words. His eyes gazed over Goose into the distance of the vast wilderness. Goose whimpered.

Clarence let out a long sigh. His shoulders slumped, and he seemed to droop on the stump. "I don't know what to do," he said as his eyes looked down at the forest floor, and his head shook almost imperceptibly from side to side. Then he lifted his gaze and looked at Goose, his eyes settling to rest squarely on the buckskin dog. They narrowed, and he seemed to study Goose. Goose looked away uncomfortably.

In the evening, Clarence stacked logs in the campfire and pressed the remnants of an old, yellow newspaper beneath them. He bent over and rolled his thumb down the wheel of a lighter, and the yellow flame lapped at the dried edges of paper and soon grew. The dark night of the forest lit in a soft amber hue. Goose lay a short distance from the fire and watched Clarence take a long stick and poke the newspaper under the logs and then stir the fire over and over again. Soon, the flames licked upward, the logs caught fire, and the area around the cabin glowed. Clarence stepped away and dropped into a folding, fabric camping chair. His weight sagged on the aluminum poles, and he leaned backward, lifting his gaze toward the small patch of open sky that watched them from above, the stars twinkling like eyes.

For a long time, the two sat by the fire in silence. Clarence stared ahead into the flames, their wisps dancing and crackling against the thick logs. Then, in the distance to his left, Goose heard the crunching of leaves and rose quickly to his feet. His body tensed, and his head lowered, his eyes peering into the darkness. The muscles on his shoulders and thighs rippled as he stared into the forest. Clarence shifted in his seat and looked, although Goose could feel that he was not alarmed.

Slowly, Goose began to growl, casting the menace of his voice deep into the forest at whatever predator lurked within. He dipped his head lower, his eyes adjusting to the night, and he scanned the forest.

"It's ok, Goose," said Clarence from behind him, his voice soft and warm. "It's ok," he said again.

THE DOG IN THE HOLLOW

As his eyes adjusted to the night, Goose could make out forms in the forest. The trunks of trees grew in his vision like grayish sentinels standing behind a dark shroud. In their midst, he could see a ghostly figure staring at him, its narrow eyes glowing in the darkness.

"It's only Fenton," said Clarence softly from behind him.

Goose stared back into the woods and squinted his eyes. He studied the specter in the forest, long and lean, the nub of his front paw lifted gently. Slowly, Goose rested on his haunches, and his curled lips settled.

Behind him, he could feel Clarence staring out into the dark forest and could sense a tide of emotion surging within.

Clarence spoke softly as he looked fondly upon Fenton in the shadows. "Even the wild ones need somebody every now and then."

CHAPTER 9

As the narrow rays of sun filtered through the tiny cracks in the cabin, Goose stirred in his bed. He'd slept little the night before. For hours, he tossed and turned on the stack of blankets, twisting and shifting to find a position in which his mind would rest. No matter how many times he stood, adjusted himself, then crumpled back down to the blankets with a huff, his thoughts would not stop racing.

He knew that miles below through the thick forest, the others huddled against the dark night in plastic barrels deep in the hollow. Over and over again, he envisioned Delilah's dingy white fur slumping limply to the ground, the life that once filled her draining away into the black night. The thoughts made him shudder, and he replayed the scene again and again.

His mind was filled with the blinding glare of the stark white lights inside the trailer, and he could smell the dank sweat and pungent tobacco of the men. He could hear their raucous cheers as Rebel tore into him again and again. He could feel the Man's wiry fingers digging into his underbelly as he carried him back to his barrel and dumped him on the ground to die. And he could feel the darkness of night that loomed above the hollow, soaking into him and threatening to consume him.

As the morning rays pushed through the cracks of the cabin, Goose embraced them. Though tired and weary, he pushed his mind toward thoughts of being alive and safe, with a soft bed and a new friend. Soon, the dark thoughts receded into the corners of his mind, at least for the time being.

For a long while, he sat there in the corner, his chin resting on his paws, waiting for Clarence to arise. Silently, his eyes scanned the bed for any signs of movement, but Clarence lay like a heap, mentally and physically exhausted. Outside, he could hear the gentle flutelike whistle of thrushes in the morning. Finally, Goose saw the old blanket rustle, and Clarence rolled over in the bed. His eyes remained closed, and his face was pinched tight as if troubling thoughts filled his mind as well.

Softly, almost imperceptibly, Goose let out a single whimper.

Slowly, like curtains being drawn by a steady hand, Clarence's eyelids opened, and he looked down into the corner of the cabin at Goose, who sat upright now, staring back at him. In the shadows of the old structure, split by rays of sun that lanced through the small cracks between the wood, the two gazed at each other, each seeking to know what swirled within the other.

Finally, Clarence leaned into the mattress, bracing his elbow against the worn cushion, and pushed himself up. The blanket fell from his shoulders, revealing a slender frame punctuated by the sharp angles of his bones.

"Good morning," was all he said, flatly. Goose could not read his emotions.

Clarence leaned forward on the bed, rested his elbows on his knees, and pressed his knuckles into his eyes. He groaned softly, and then his mouth opened into a large yawn. Goose rested silently in the corner, although his posture showed he was alert, ready to rise at the command.

Clarence sat there on the edge of the bed for a long time, staring blankly at the wall. Finally, he turned and looked back at Goose with his lips open and his eyes looking as if he might say something. But then, they closed, and he was silent for a while longer. In the corner, Goose lowered his head somberly and rested it on his paws. His eyes rolled downward, and he stared at the floor.

"We're going to town today."

THE DOG IN THE HOLLOW

Clarence's tone was firm and decisive, but beneath it, Goose could sense a bubbling fear. Goose lifted his head and looked at Clarence; the energy sprang back into the dog, and slowly, tentatively, the tip of his tail began to wag like a pendulum.

"You up for another walk, friend?" said Clarence, now looking down at Goose. His eyes were narrowed, and Goose could feel the compassion creeping into his voice.

Goose rose to his feet quickly, stumbling just slightly as his paw caught in the corner of the blanket. He barked sharply just once.

Yes.

Soon, Clarence had packed a small backpack with two small bottles of water and some snacks for their trip. He rested it on the bed and then walked to the shelf, studying the books that were stacked neatly against the cabin wall. One by one, he pulled out three books, his slender fingers pulling the top of the book downward at an angle. Then he took them with his left hand, slid them carefully into the backpack, and then zipped it tight.

He slung it over his shoulder and turned to Goose. "You coming?" Once more, Goose could feel something unsettled within Clarence.

As they stepped from the cabin, Clarence started into the woods, heading in the opposite direction of the hollow. Goose stopped in his tracks, planting his feet, but Clarence continued. When Clarence reached the end of the clearing and stepped into the woods, Goose barked sharply.

Clarence stopped, his feet crunching on the dry leaves, and he turned, looking puzzled. "You're not coming now?" he said, his brow furrowing.

Goose barked again, and Clarence studied him from the patchy shadows of the forest. Then, Goose turned and trotted to the other edge of the clearing slowly, allowing Clarence to follow him. When he reached the edge, he turned over his shoulder and looked back at Clarence, who looked back somewhat impatiently.

Clarence stood there for a moment and then spoke. "I know, Goose. I haven't forgotten them," he said, his voice becoming tender. "But I can't do it by myself."

His words were laced with profound sadness, and Goose knew then that Clarence would not follow him, not now. Slowly, he turned and began to lope back toward the man. Halfway across the clearing, his trot turned into a gallop, and he ran to Clarence's side. He sensed he could trust the man, and together, the two headed off into the woods.

Throughout the day, the man and dog ventured through the thick forest, picking their way through the low brush as the mountain sloped downward.

THE DOG IN THE HOLLOW

Clarence walked at an angle to the grade of the mountain, stepping carefully and leaning backward against his momentum. Step by step, they followed the rays of light that stabbed through the forest canopy and made their way toward the town that lay below.

As the sun crested high in the sky, the ground began to flatten, and they tread across a flat stretch of forest in silence, only their feet crunching in the leaves. Goose could sense that Clarence grew more and more anxious with every step. Far ahead, Goose could make out light pressing into the forest, and the trees seemed to open. Soon, he heard the sounds of cars racing past and the dirty flicker of grit and gravel spitting off the sides of the road from their spinning wheels. Before long, the two emerged from the forest and stood on the back side of a rusted guardrail with the cracked, gray asphalt of a mountain road just before them.

Clarence pulled the backpack tighter and looked either way on the road. To the right, the sounds of an engine loomed up and around the bend, and soon, the dull, rusted blue of a diesel dump truck appeared in the distance, roaring toward them. Clarence stepped backward, lowering his hand to wave Goose back toward the tree. As the truck passed, Goose looked up and saw the grizzled beard of the driver as his face turned and looked down at the motley pair from high up in the cab, his gaze quizzical. As the truck roared past, Clarence lifted his leg and stepped over the guardrail and then the other until he was standing on the other side.

He turned and looked down at Goose, who suddenly felt so small exposed to the world. "Can you make it over?" Clarence said. Goose sat there looking back at him, unsure of what to do.

Clarence reached down and patted the guardrail with his hand. As he did, he looked over his shoulder left and right. "Come on," he said. "Up."

Goose whimpered and stepped up the gentle slope and sniffed at Clarence's fingers. "Come on," he said again. Goose paused for a moment and then quickly sprang up on his back legs and rested his paws on the guardrail. The narrow edge of rusted metal dug into his paws.

In the distance, Goose heard the sound of another engine coming up the slope from the left. Clarence's eyes widened, and he reached his hands into the pits of Goose's legs and pulled him forward. Goose pushed off with his back legs and leapt over the guardrail, landing beside the road.

Clarence looked to his left, toward the sound of the engine. "Come on!" he shouted and then sprinted across the cracked pavement. Goose ran after him. On the other side, Clarence stopped and stood in the tall grass and weeds that separated the road from the gray craggy cliffs that loomed above. Behind them, a car passed, whipping around the bend and continuing up the slope of the mountain.

When it had passed, Clarence turned and started along the road, heading down the slope the way the car had come. Goose followed, and for some time, the two walked with the occasional car whipping past them, but he felt safe, away from the dangerous road.

At last, the road began to flatten, and the craggy rocks dwindled to small, low boulders. As the slope dissipated, the road bent and straightened. Beside Goose, Clarence stopped. Goose looked up and gazed down the straight stretch. To his right, a rusted green sign on a battered metal post simply said "Mayfield" and beneath it "Population 968."

A few hundred yards ahead, the grayish pavement and its dull yellow line morphed from a twisted mountain road into the main street of the small town. Goose gazed ahead at a series of small, squatty brick buildings, some covered with chipped white paint. Bland, striped awnings stretched off the side of the worn buildings, and flashing neon from dated lights beckoned wearily at anyone passing by.

Beside him, Clarence breathed deeply, and

Goose could feel his heart racing. For a moment, the man seemed to wobble, but then he righted himself. He looked down at Goose, and his eyes bore a sadness that the dog had never seen before. Then he looked back up toward the town, inhaled, and began to walk toward the edge of Mayfield.

CHAPTER 10

At the edge of town, the rocky, gravel shoulder ended abruptly, fading unceremoniously into the cracked, pale concrete of a sidewalk that showed scars of decades of mountain weather. Side by side, the bedraggled pair trudged along toward the buildings that drew closer and closer with each step. Clarence pulled at the straps of his backpack and lowered his head, his greasy hair swinging over his forehead like a curtain. Beside him and just a pace behind, Goose stepped cautiously, bewildered at the sights and sounds of this place.

Up ahead and to the right, a chime rang and a shop door creaked open. Goose stopped in his tracks at the sound and leaned backward, hesitant. Clarence noticed and stopped as well, lifting his head from the sidewalk. From the doorway, a lively younger man in a royal purple t-shirt stepped down to the sidewalk. In his arms, he carried a small grocery bag with bottles clinking inside. Then, a younger woman stepped out onto the sidewalk, flipping her long, blonde hair over her shoulder. Seeing Clarence and Goose just feet away, she startled. She looked down at Goose, and her nose sneered up instinctively. She stepped back up the ledge into the store. The young man stepped in front of her defensively.

"Professor Crandall?" came the woman's voice from the doorway, sounding incredulous. She was squinting and staring down at him from the doorstep, a troubled expression on her face.

Next to her, the man gazed straight into Clarence's face. His mouth fell agape. "Are you....?" he started to ask but could not finish.

Clarence looked up briefly, his stringy hair falling on either side of his gaunt face. His mouth opened as if to say something, and then he bowed his head awkwardly, nodded quickly, then hustled past the door, reaching down to guide Goose past. Goose pressed against Clarence's leg, bending his body to avoid the man whose head turned and gawked at them as they passed.

The two shuffled down the sidewalk. Behind them, Goose could hear their voices.

"Jesus," said the young man, the tone of disgust apparent in his voice. "He's a wreck," he said and then chuckled lightly. At the words, Clarence increased his pace.

The two figures continued hustling down the sidewalk, passing in front of the windows of small shops. Goose occasionally looked up as they passed, marveling at the sight of wares in the windows of the various stores—antique nightstands and sewing machines, brightly colored boxes of food and fresh produce, shirts and hats in the same royal purple the young man had worn, bottles with different colored liquids, and all sorts of wondrous things.

Beside them, the occasional car passed down the center street, headed toward the mountains. The mix of loud music, squeaking metal parts, and the indistinct chatter of people filled the air all around them.

After several blocks, Clarence stepped in front of Goose and turned to the right. "This way," he said hurriedly and then continued down the side of an old brick building, its surface absent any windows. The road sloped uphill and curved slightly to the left. Goose trotted along, keeping pace with Clarence.

Just ahead, a single-story building of thick, yellowed brick stood with weathered gray shingles stretching over a shaded porch. On one of the columns, a once-ornate sign was nailed. The slender, curved letters said "Mayfield Public

Library."

Clarence hurried up toward the front porch and stopped at the bottom of a short set of stairs. He looked behind them as if making sure no one was following them. Then he scanned the porch and the ragged grass lawn that grew out before it. His mind seemed in turmoil as if an important decision brewed within him.

Finally, he looked down at Goose and spoke. "Stay right here. I'll be back in one second," he said in almost a whisper. Goose looked up at him. Then, Clarence took a step up on the porch, and Goose moved to follow.

Clarence put his hand up, his palm facing Goose. "Stay here," he said, his words firm but pained. Then without waiting to see Goose's reaction, he turned and walked up the steps, sliding the backpack off his shoulder as he did and pulling at the zippers in a single motion. As he reached the door, his hand withdrew the books he had packed. He grabbed the handle of the screen door and pulled. The old hinges creaked and groaned, and then Clarence disappeared behind the flapping door.

Goose stared after him and whimpered, but he did not move. He knew what Clarence meant. After a moment, he lowered his haunches and sat in the grass, facing the door. His mouth opened, and his pink tongue extended into a light pant. Behind the door, he could hear Clarence's muted voice speaking with a woman.

Just then, he heard the crunch of rocks beneath tires. He could smell the burning oil from an engine and the noise of gears turning filled his ears. He stood suddenly and turned.

His eyes gazed upon the shining white hood of a car. Atop, blue lights twinkled, sending flashes into Goose's eyes that caused him to wince and turn away. He heard a door open, and then the sound of boots on the asphalt. As he looked up and through the shimmering lights, he saw a tall, lean figure, his hair blonde and closely cropped. His tan uniform was every bit as crisp and orderly as Clarence's clothes were disheveled. The man looked over the hood at Goose, and his right hand reached down to his side. Goose could see him unbuttoning a pistol from its holster, and then his hand rested on the gun's butt.

"Stay in the car," said the man's voice through the open driver's door to someone else inside. Goose looked up but could not see through the reflections of the library that splayed across the windshield in distorted hues of brown and yellow.

The man continued to stare down at Goose and tilted his head to the right, angling his mouth toward a radio receiver attached high on his shoulder. "Unit 12, arrived at location. We might need Animal Control," he said, his words cold.

Goose's mouth hung open wide, and he began to pant harder, uncertain at the scene. Then, behind him, he heard the door of the library creak open again, and he heard panicked footsteps scurry across the porch.

"He's mine," said Clarence, nearly out of breath. "He's friendly," he assured the man whose hand still rested on the gun.

For a long moment, there was silence as the two men gazed at each other. Goose could feel the racing of Clarence's heart behind him, and the anxiety made his fur ripple.

"Afternoon, Clarence," said the man with the gun, his words dripping with disdain.

Clarence said nothing.

"To what do we owe this distinct pleasure," continued the man with the gun.

Clarence stumbled with his words. His head bowed. "Just returning some books," he said, the words trailing away into the sounds of the car's running motor.

The officer's lips tightened and curled. His eyes dropped, and he looked down at Goose. "Got a call about a suspicious person and an aggressive dog," he said, nodding at Goose with the final words. "Didn't expect to find you here."

THE DOG IN THE HOLLOW

"The dog's not aggressive, Hinton," said Clarence. His head was bowed, but there was no mistaking the defiance in his voice.

Deputy Hinton looked at Clarence and then down at Goose. His lips seemed to smile now. "Finally got yourself a friend." He chuckled softly.

Just then, the passenger's door swung open slowly, almost hesitantly. Goose looked up across the hood, and he could see a figure moving. A slender woman with long, blonde hair rested her hand above the window frame and pulled herself up from the seat. She stood there behind the door, staring out at the scene. Goose studied her. Her pale blue eyes looked upon Clarence with something deeper than pity, but he couldn't place it. Her face was framed by long locks of hair that fell to her shoulders, resting on a soft, white blouse. Hinton turned and looked at her, his hand never moving from the butt of the gun.

"Clarence," said the woman, almost desperately, as if pleading to someone lost. "Clarence," she repeated, and Goose could feel the depth of sorrow in her words. The corners of her eyes grew moist.

Clarence lifted his head and looked at her. His dead eyes stared through her, but deep inside him, the emotions welled. Goose saw his chest sink suddenly as if to catch his breath. Then, Clarence lowered his head.

"Loretta," was all he said, and then his gaze lowered again.

"Are you....?" she started. Then she tried again. "Are you, ok?"

Clarence only nodded without looking at her.

Hinton turned from Loretta to Clarence after a moment. "Can't be walking a dog around here without a leash, Clarence," he scolded him. "I could take your friend here to the pound..." he said, looking down at Goose "...and write you up a ticket."

"Glen!" said the woman suddenly, turning to look at the deputy. He looked away, almost ashamed.

Clarence composed himself and looked up. His eyes fell on her with deep resolve. Then he turned and looked at the deputy. "I'm here to see the Sheriff," he said coldly.

Hinton looked incredulous and then chortled softly. "What do you need to see the Sheriff about, Clarence?" He sneered at him. "Somebody come and stole all your liquor?"

Loretta turned at the deputy and hissed at him. "Stop it!"

"I need to see the Sheriff," was all Clarence said. "We're headed there now, then we'll be gone." Clarence reached into his backpack and pulled out a length of old clothesline and quickly fashioned a loop. Then he stooped over and looped it over Goose's head, and it fell gently around the base of his thick chest. He tugged at it once, urging Goose forward.

"We'll be on our way, and then you won't see us again," said Clarence. He tugged again at the clothesline and then started down the short road back toward town. Goose followed.

As he passed Deputy Hinton, he gave a wide berth and stared down the entire time. Hinton only turned his head and watched Clarence and Goose pass, his hand never leaving the butt of the gun. Goose could feel the woman's eyes upon them as they rounded the curving road back toward town.

CHAPTER 11

C larence walked briskly down the block, tugging occasionally at the clothesline. Goose didn't seem to know what to make of the strange tether; he had known only heavy chains around his neck, but this line seemed light and almost buoyant, although he could sense Clarence's tension through it. Clarence hustled along; his boots scuffed the pavement, and a bead of sweat drew across his forehead. Goose could sense the turmoil swirling in his mind.

The pair continued down the block of the small town, passing shop after shop with their tall glass panes framing stacks of clothing, furniture, and other wares. Purple and gold ribbons adorned each light post, the same colors on the young man's shirt from earlier. When they reached a street corner a few blocks down, Clarence stopped. Goose could feel the rush of adrenaline in his body, could see his temples pulsing, and could feel his urge to turn around and look behind them, but he did not. Nor did Goose, who stood with his mouth open from the hurried pace, looking upward at Clarence, waiting for his direction.

Clarence seemed to scan the intersection, looking up and down both the streets that cut through the center of town. He squinted and looked to the right, his eyes surveying the cracked asphalt that sloped gently up into a neighborhood with single-story, weathered brick houses where large canopies of trees cast shadows through the small yards. Finally, Clarence turned and headed up the street as if recognizing something.

"This way," was all he said to Goose, not turning back. His mind was elsewhere.

Goose followed him to the right until the sidewalk ended, and the two stepped down over the curb and walked along the edge of the street. Clarence turned over his shoulder nervously, looking for Hinton, but he was nowhere to be seen. Together, they walked past nearly a dozen houses that lined the small street. Although old and worn, the houses were well-kept, ranging from sturdy ranchers to petite cottages. Occasionally, Goose could feel eyes upon them from porches and windows, and he sensed that Clarence could feel them too, but he did not acknowledge them.

After a short walk, Clarence stopped in the

street and looked to the left. There, set off from the road, a tiny, pale-yellow cottage sat among a cluster of brick houses and stands of oak trees. The sun danced through the leaves and cast mottled patterns on the roof. A small blue car sat in the gravel driveway. Clarence looked left and then crossed the street with Goose following him.

As he got to the edge of the driveway, he stopped and took a deep breath. He looked down and then up again at the house, studying the thin metal numbers on the teal door. Then, he leaned down and pulled the clothesline snug around Goose's neck.

Goose's skin trembled for a moment, and he grew weary. He suddenly feared that Clarence was going to leave him, to abandon him. Goose could feel this short, rich life slipping away from him. His warm spot on the cabin floor, the sounds of the forest, the scraps of food so gently laid by Clarence all began to vanish in his mind. He began to whimper, and then the whimper turned to a long, quiet whine.

Clarence looked down at him. "It's ok," he said. But his eyes looked troubled. Goose didn't believe him and let out a sharp bark as he stared back at him.

"Shhhhhh," Clarence hissed as if embarrassed. But Goose barked again. "Shhhhhh," Clarence said louder and with more urgency.

Then, the teal door creaked and began to open slowly. Goose could feel the fright surge through Clarence's body, and he stood upright, staring at the door like a ghost. Goose turned and looked with him.

The slender face of a woman appeared at the door. She was slightly older than Clarence, and long lines creased her face. Her gray hair was pulled back into a ponytail, and she looked kind and wise, but inquisitive. She poked her head out, her eyes studying the edge of her driveway. Goose could sense Clarence gulp.

"Clarence?" said the woman, her tone one of distinct surprise. "Clarence Crandall? Is that you?" she said. Goose could hear the tenderness creep into her voice. She stepped out of the door and stood on the low concrete porch, a dark shawl around her shoulders. A pair of rounded eyeglasses hung from her neck. She reached down and lifted them, placing them over her eyes.

"Hello, Margaret," said Clarence. His voice was nervous but warm. Goose stood there, his head swiveling slowly between the two of them. Clarence stepped forward a half pace.

"My God," said the woman. Her mouth began to form a smile, and she stepped down off the concrete porch and came toward them. "Clarence," she said. This time the warmth was obvious in her tone. She walked toward him, and several feet away, she raised her slight arms and extended them toward him, welcoming him into her embrace.

Clarence shambled forward, and Goose could feel the nervousness fade from him into a gentle sadness. "It's good to see you, Margaret," he said tenderly. The two embraced, and Clarence sank his head into her shoulder, his arm still limply holding the clothesline. After a moment, they released the embrace and stood there looking at each other.

"I'm so glad to see you, Clarence," said Margaret. Goose could see the corners of her eye glistening. Clarence bowed his head. For the first time, Margaret looked down at Goose, and she lowered her eyeglasses. Her mouth and her eyes smiled. "Who do you have here?" she said with a warm inflection in her voice that helped calm Goose. His tail began to wag side to side.

"This is my new friend, Goose," said Clarence, looking down. "He found me somehow up the hill," he said, gesturing vaguely back toward the mountain.

Margaret said nothing but only smiled kindly down at Goose. Her hands were bundled together in front of her like a child waiting patiently for a present.

"Margaret," said Clarence, a tone of seriousness

creeping into his voice. "I'm sorry to ask this of you," he said and then paused.

Margaret looked up at him, and the smile seemed to fade. Again, she waited patiently.

"I have something I need to do in town. I was wondering...." he stammered and paused. After a moment, he continued. "I was wondering if you wouldn't mind letting me leave him in your backyard for just a bit," he said at last.

Margaret studied Clarence. Goose sensed her concern was for the man, not his request. "Why don't you both come in for a while, Clarence?"

Clarence looked down, but Margaret kept her eyes on him.

"I'll make you both something to eat. We can chat, and then you can go to town," she said, more of a request than a question.

Clarence seemed to sway on his feet. Finally, he spoke quietly. "That would be great, Margaret."

For the next hour, Clarence, Goose, and Margaret sat around her living room. Goose lay on an old dog bed in the middle of the room, resting comfortably after lapping down a large can of dog food served to him in a metal bowl. He could smell the scents of the other dogs, the ones he heard Margaret usher into the backyard before he and Clarence came in. He hadn't seen them, but he could hear their tags jingling happily, and he knew them from the tufts of fur they left behind. He could tell they were loved.

On either side of him, Margaret and Clarence talked quietly.

"We miss you at the school, Clarence," she said. Her eyes looked downward longingly.

Clarence said nothing, and Goose could feel the sadness well inside him.

"I wish you hadn't left as you did. I would have supported you. You know that." She paused and studied him. "Professor Gentry, Dean Williams, many of us would have supported you, Clarence," she added. "We could have gotten you help," she said gingerly.

"I know, Margaret, I know," was all he could say. The room was silent for a long time.

Margaret spoke again. "Some of your students still ask about you."

"I saw some of them at the store," said Clarence dismissively.

"They're not all like that," retorted Margaret. "You were a wonderful professor, Clarence, and they know that," she said. "We all have our travails."

Clarence sat back in his chair and looked out the large bay window in the living room. Outside, the leaves seemed to twist and dance in the early afternoon wind.

THE DOG IN THE HOLLOW

"I saw her downtown," said Clarence.

Margaret looked down at the floor, and her face grew long and serious.

"She was with him. Still together," he said. "I guess it was meant to be after all." Goose could feel the sadness welling inside him once more.

Margaret spoke tenderly. "You're better than them, Clarence." There was a long pause. "I believe in you," she said, and the words resonated in the quiet room. Outside, the jingle of frolicking dogs floated in the air. "I hope you've found some peace in the woods."

Clarence looked down again at the floor, and his mind seemed to turn inward. "I have," he said somberly. His voice was sincere. "I have, Margaret," he said again.

Goose looked between the two of them. He lay there quiet and calm, but his ears were alert at their words. Clarence sensed him listening and turned his head toward him, and their eyes connected.

"I see that you have," said Margaret. A small smile creased her face as she looked down at Goose.

"Margaret," said Clarence, his tone becoming purposeful. "I have to go see the Sheriff about something."

Margaret looked up, and her brow furrowed. "What's going on, Clarence?"

Clarence thought in silence for some time. After

a long pause, he began to talk, telling Margaret what he had seen in the woods. As the words came from his mouth, her expression grew more and more concerned. She leaned forward in her chair, her voice attuned to his every word. When he was finished, her mouth was open, but she had no words.

"I have to go see the Sheriff," Clarence said resolutely, and he rose from his chair. "Will you take care of Goose for an hour or so while I do?" he said. "They won't let me bring him in the station if Hinton has anything to do with it, and I'm not stringing him to some light post."

Margaret rose from her seat. She walked toward Clarence, her small feet standing just beside Goose. She reached down and took his hand. "I will, Clarence," she said, looking into his eyes. "But I want you to promise me you'll be careful." She squeezed his hand tighter.

Clarence looked down at the floor and then up at her. "I will," he said, his tone grave.

She held his hand for a moment longer and then released it. "Go do what you need to do, Clarence. He will be just fine here," she said as she looked down warmly at Goose.

CHAPTER 12

Clarence's mind wandered as he shuffled down the cracked pavement toward Mayfield's main street. His steps felt slow and hesitant as if somehow the deed ahead resisted him. Or perhaps what he had left behind drew him back.

His mind conjured faint memories of the Sheriff's station, the small innocuous brick building that sat on the far end of the main street. He'd been there just once before when his world came crashing down, and his memories of the place were vague yet unpleasant.

He could hear the voices of the college students before he reached the intersection, boisterous and carefree. He could hear their jests and flirtations; they fluttered down the street and evaporated into the warmth of the late-summer day. Ahead, he saw shadows forming in the street, and they drew near, growing larger. Clarence paused on the side street and stood motionless, hoping they would not see him.

From around the corner, four young people appeared, side by side in a line, two men and two women. The couples held hands as they walked abreast, stepping into the street. One of the men turned his head and saw Clarence standing there. He squinted, peering into the shadow that fell from the building. The woman turned and then clutched his hand harder, pulling a satchel full of large books that Clarence knew to be college textbooks closer to her. The four hurried along, and Clarence waited until they passed before he stepped from the shadows into the sunlight that splashed across the main street.

He breathed deeply, exposed again to the world. Then, he tucked his head and turned to his right, stepping purposefully down the street in the direction of the station. Ahead, he could see the four young adults, their shapes bobbing up and down with laughter and the playful antics of college students savoring their last moments before the beginning of the fall semester.

Clarence knew their sounds and demeanor well. Before his exile in the woods, he had visited the same bookstore, placing textbook orders with the manager, completing forms, and chatting about the semester to come. Now, he slinked behind the students, a motley shadow.

As he passed the windows of the storefronts that lined the street, he kept his head down, avoiding glimpses of his reflection in the window. He pulled the backpack tighter over his shoulder as if the embrace of the straps would comfort him through this moment.

Soon, the storefronts ended, and Clarence continued down the pale sidewalk that bent and wound around a curve. On his right, a small white church sat behind a chain-link fence.

As he rounded the curve, he lifted his head, and he could see it. A hundred yards ahead stood a small, squatty brick building with a roof of gray shingles that sloped backward. On the face of the building, two glass doors greeted him, swathed with various written signs beneath an ornate and official-looking crest that seemed misplaced on the otherwise mundane building. Clarence paused for a moment there in the gravel parking lot.

He inhaled deeply and could feel himself trembling. His mind began to race, and he could sense the lingering fear creep into his brain, telling him to turn and run, to retrieve Goose, and go back to the woods. He took a step backward with his left foot, and his knee bent to pivot and turn. But he did not. He stood there in the parking lot beneath the warm sun as cars occasionally wound the corner and disappeared down the road that led further into the mountains.

Once more, he breathed in. His chest rose, and he began to feel whole once more. The churn in his mind started to subside, and now he could clearly see the reason he had come. In his mind, he could hear the snap-crack of the gunshot, and he remembered the dog crumbling lifelessly to the ground. As he stood there at the edge of town, he could hear the whimpers of the chained dogs at the edge of the hollow. But most of all, he could see Goose, clear in his mind. He remembered the horrible punctures and the swollen wounds and could feel the dog's purpose course through him. Now it was his purpose, too.

He drew himself upright and began to walk toward the double glass doors. Beneath him, the gravel crunched and the wind tousled the unkempt hairs of his beard. He reached the doors and extended his hand to grab the aluminum handle just below the gold-colored signage that read "Mayfield Sherriff's Office." He pulled on the door and entered, savoring the chilled air that engulfed him.

As he stepped into the small lobby, a voice rose over a microphone. "Can I help you?" said a woman's voice, cold and unwelcoming. Clarence looked up, and he could see the woman sitting at a counter behind a thick Plexiglas barrier. Without pause, her voice crackled through the round speaker just before him. "Can I help you, sir?" she said, this time more impatiently.

Clarence looked at her befuddled. "Yes, yes..." he said, stumbling for words. The woman pursed her lips, and her face tightened.

"I...I need to speak with the Sheriff," said Clarence. He knew the trepidation in his words would not help.

"What is it about?" she asked curtly.

Clarence struggled for the words. He hadn't thought to formulate how he might phrase his strange inquiry. "I...I have something to report," was all he could muster.

Almost before he was finished, the woman placed her palm on a paper form and thrust it forward, sliding the document into a small tray below the speaker. "Fill out this form, and I'll give it to a deputy," she said. She dropped a pen into the tray, and it clattered, rolled, and finally fell still.

Clarence stood there staring at the form. For a moment, he said nothing. He could feel the woman's impatience.

"No. I need to speak to the Sheriff personally," he said, his voice resolute.

"The Sheriff doesn't see visitors."

Clarence was flustered. This wasn't going as he

expected. "Please," he pleaded, sounding desperate. "I...I..." he looked down at the form again. "I don't trust that it will reach him," he said.

Her brow furrowed in frustration, and her mouth began to open. Clarence could already hear the bitterness in her unspoken words.

"I don't mean you, mam," he offered meekly. "It's just...it's just very important that I speak to him," he said.

At that moment, he heard the door opening behind him and the shuffling of feet entering the lobby. Then, he heard the jingle of keys and the rustle of equipment, and he knew without turning who it was.

"Look who it is," said Deputy Hinton. "I see you've found your way here," he scoffed.

Clarence tensed and then turned around and faced the deputy. His chin rose, and he looked him square in the eye.

"You lose that mongrel of yours?" mocked Hinton. His lips twisted into a smirk.

"I need to see the Sheriff, Glen," said Clarence directly. "I know you don't care for me, but I have something serious to report, and then I'll be on my way."

Hinton's hand lowered, and his palm rested on the butt of the holstered pistol on his right. His smirk faded, and his face grew stern. "Sheriff doesn't take visitors, Clarence. Whatever you've got to say, you can say it to me."

Behind Clarence, the door opened briskly. Clarence turned suddenly and saw a tall, older man standing in the doorway. Dark, wire-framed glasses sat up high on his nose, and his face and physique were chiseled and military-like. "What's going on out here?" he asked gruffly.

Hinton seemed to melt slightly, and his posture softened. "Sheriff, Clarence here says he has something to report but doesn't seem to want to tell anyone about it."

Clarence glanced at Hinton and then back at the Sheriff. Seizing the moment, he spoke, his voice confident but cordial. "Sheriff Jefferson, I'm sorry to bother you like this, but I have something I need to share with you, something about a crime."

Sheriff Jefferson stood in the doorway measuring Clarence with his eyes. Behind the Plexiglas, the stern woman looked on, clearly engrossed in the excitement of an otherwise mundane day in Mayfield. Jefferson clenched his jaw and looked Clarence up and down for a moment.

"Come in then," he said and then turned to head down a short hallway that led to his office.

Without hesitation, Clarence stepped forward, reaching for the door and catching it just before it swung closed. He could hear Hinton behind him, bearing down. Clarence stepped quickly behind the Sheriff down the short hall and then turned a sharp left into a corner office on the backside of the building.

"Sit down," ordered Jefferson, gesturing to a pair of hard wooden chairs before the broad, deep brown desk.

For the next ten minutes, Clarence talked uninterrupted. He talked of Goose's arrival, the wounds he had endured, and then of their travels to the hollow. He described its location in great detail, including the circle of chained dogs, the trailer, the small house, and the Man. He told them how the Man killed the dog, and he watched their faces carefully for sympathy or interest.

He found none.

When he was finished, he rested his hands on his knees. "Sheriff, those dogs need help," he pleaded. From behind the desk, Sheriff Jefferson looked back at him, his face rigid and emotionless as if chiseled from granite. Hinton stood just inside the door, hovering over Clarence. His face bore a look of disgust.

The room was silent for a long moment, and then Sheriff Jefferson spoke. "Clarence, you know better than I do that we have school starting here in less than a week." He paused for a moment, studying Clarence's reaction, and then continued. "We're about to have drunk college kids, parties, laptop thefts, and a whole bunch of other trouble we need to deal with." He paused for a moment, looking at Clarence with what almost resembled pity. "You made all this fuss to come here and tell me to take my few deputies and go save some dogs out in the woods?"

Hinton shook his head in disgust. "I'll escort you out, Clarence," he said and then leaned down and grasped Clarence's arm. Clarence tensed and pulled away, his eyes darting sideways to Hinton. Hinton's hand lowered again to the butt of his pistol.

"Settle down, you two," said Sheriff Jefferson. "I'm not having this beef in my office," he said. Hinton relaxed slightly. "Clarence," he said, his head looking down, and for a moment, the words sounded patronizing. "I don't know what you've been doing up in those woods, and I don't want to know."

Clarence pressed his lips together, and his nostrils flared.

"But whatever it is," continued Sheriff Jefferson, "you keep it up there and don't bring your troubles back to this town," he said. "We've had enough of it." His eyes grew icy and bored into Clarence. Then he looked at Hinton and nodded toward the door.

Hinton reached out to grab his arm, but Clarence pulled away. He bent his knees and stood, pushing the chair back swiftly. Without a word, he turned and headed for the door, brushing past Hinton without a word.

Soon, he was back in front of Margaret's yellow cottage. The short walk had not quelled his anger, and he could feel the blood pulsing through his veins. He knocked firmly on the door and, in response, heard Goose's sharp barking and the sound of his claws racing across the wooden floor. He looked through the glass window and saw the dog rush into the living room, his eyes on the door and his tail swishing from left to right. After a moment, Margaret came to greet him; her expression was warm and tender. She took his hand gently and led him in, guiding him to the sofa. Goose rushed between his legs, his big blocky head pressing hard into his thighs as his butt wiggled ferociously, his tail threatening to send Margaret's nearby decorations and ornaments crashing about the floor.

"How did it go?" she asked him gently. It was clear from her tone that she did not expect much.

Clarence reached down, and his hands caressed Goose's bony skull. He could feel the dog's warm tongue lapping at his palm, and he could feel the boundless love course through his body.

"I'm going to have to take care of it myself," he said grimly.

CHAPTER 13

Goose tugged at the clothesline, pulling Clarence along. Both man and dog ducked their heads and hurried through the town, stepping quickly down the main street. Behind shop windows and in doorways, curious faces watched the strange pair. As they approached a corner, Clarence lifted his gaze to look for traffic and saw a small group of college students standing there. He recognized several of them and instinctively moved toward the edge of the sidewalk, searching for cars. Goose followed him, zigzagging on the taut leash into the back of Clarence's legs, causing him to stumble.

Clarence could feel the student's eyes boring into him, and without looking in their direction, he knew their faces were contorted in embarrassment for him. He stepped off the curb and into the road, sensing no traffic. Goose hopped down after him, and just then, a flash of white rose in his periphery to the right. He looked up, and his breath caught in his throat.

The patrol car pressed the brakes somewhat dramatically, and the police cruiser skidded slightly on the loose gravel until it pulled beside Clarence and Goose, blocking their path across the road. Hinton turned on his lights, clearly intending to make a spectacle of the scene before the throngs of bystanders on the sidewalks and in the shops. His siren chirped once. Then he leaned out the window, placing his left elbow against the outside of the door. With his right hand, he pulled his sunglasses down on the bridge of his nose.

"You ever heard of a crosswalk, Clarence?" he asked, smirking.

Clarence stood with his head bowed. Beside him, Goose panted and paced in the street, tugging at the end of the rope.

Hinton pulled his glasses off and stared at Clarence as if his hard gaze could make the other man lift his chin and look him in the eye. "You heading back to the woods?" he asked.

Clarence did not respond. Goose panted loudly, anxious.

Hinton paused for a moment and then looked down thoughtfully. Then he lifted his head and spoke. "You know, Clarence..." he started. "...things worked out like they were supposed to."

He studied Clarence for a minute.

Clarence lifted his head slightly and stared into Hinton's steely eyes.

"Loretta's happy now," said Hinton. "She's got what she needs. No more playing second string to you and your books," he said, the last word carrying a hint of disgust. "She deserved more than you could give her. You should be happy for her," he said and then paused for a moment. "For us," he added, callously.

Clarence could feel the anger brewing inside of him. "Can we leave?" he asked curtly.

Hinton ignored him. "It might be time for you to move on, Clarence. Get a fresh start somewhere, leave this place behind. Know what I mean?" Hinton's eyes pressed into him.

On the sidewalk, the students gathered toward the edge of the curb to listen, trying their best not to be conspicuous by mimicking a conversation.

"You're scaring these people around here, Clarence," said Hinton, gesturing toward the sidewalk. "They see you coming into town looking like you do. They're worried what you might do. Steal from a store, go off in a drunken rage…" he said.

Clarence interrupted him sharply. "Hinton, you don't know me." The words spat from his mouth bitterly, and then there was a long, cold silence.

Hinton's lips pressed tightly together, and his face drew into a sneer. "I should write you a ticket for jaywalking, Clarence. Then take that mutt of yours and send him to the pound." He looked down at Goose, and his lips curled in disgust. "He'd probably be better off there."

Clarence stared back at him and said nothing.

"Get out of here, Clarence," he said sharply. Then, he reached up above the steering wheel and flipped off the flashing lights. The car pulled forward, and as the rear end was even with Clarence and Goose, Hinton pressed the gas and kicked up a storm of loose pebbles. Behind them, Clarence could hear the whispers of the students.

"Come on," he said and gave a gentle tug of the leash. The two crossed the road, turned down the main street, and headed out of town, their pace brisk and urgent.

Night drew slowly atop the forest as the two headed up the slope, weaving their way through dense thickets in the encroaching darkness. Above them, the glimmer of a full moon rose in the distant horizon between the cracks in the trees. Clarence had long since taken the clothesline from Goose, who now walked ahead, leading the way. In the burgeoning moonlight, Clarence could see the rippling muscles on the dog's arms as they rested on fallen trees and propelled his lean body forward toward the cabin.

Just as the sky turned an inky black, Clarence could see the faint outline of the shack not far ahead. He longed for nothing more than to lay on his bed and rest his weary feet. Soon, he was at the door with Goose just behind him. He turned the rusted knob, and the two entered—two feet and four paws. Clarence turned and flopped down on his bed, spreading his arms and savoring the throbbing of his feet as it coursed up his legs and dissipated. Goose paced in the shack for a moment and then walked to his corner, circled once, and fell down with a huff.

Then they slept for a long night, their dueling snores filling the tiny shack. Outside, Fenton howled in the near distance, but neither heard him as they dozed deep in the throes of exhaustion.

In the morning, they awoke. Clarence opened his backpack, and his eyes alighted to several cans of dog food. He forgot that Margaret had given these to him, and now his arm reached in with excitement. He pulled one out and turned to Goose, who still lay curled on his bed. When he saw the can, the dog's eyes lit up.

Together, the two sat in the corner of the cabin eating, Clarence shoveling spoonful after spoonful of cereal into his mouth. Goose opened his mouth wide and chomped at the food, taking large chunks with each bite until it was gone, and then he licked the bowl clean until it spun and then toppled off the side of his blanket bed and rattled around on the floor.

"Hungry, huh?" Clarence said, looking down at him with a slight smile.

Goose lifted his head, searching Clarence for any signs that there may be more food.

When Clarence was done, the two sat there in silence. Clarence bowed his head and rested his arms on the inside of his legs as he so often did. His shaggy hair draped down so that Goose could not see his face. In the quiet of the cabin, he wept softly.

Goose watched him and whimpered.

After a moment, Clarence raised his arm and wiped the long hair from his face. Goose could see the redness in his eyes. Then, Clarence stared straight ahead for a moment, paused, and rose to his feet.

Soon, they were headed back down the mountainside. Over his back, Clarence's rifle was slung, and his backpack was full of provisions. Goose followed, and he could sense a grim determination about Clarence as he strode purposefully through the woods toward the hollow.

For miles, the two traveled in complete silence.

Only the breaking of branches and the chirps of wrens in the high branches sounded through the forest. Occasionally, Clarence would reach back and touch the rifle as if to make sure it was still there. On one occasion, he stopped and pulled it around on its sling. He pointed the rifle to the ground and pulled back the bolt, checking the chamber. Then he placed his eye to the sight and stared with the other one closed toward the ground. When he was satisfied, he slung it back over his shoulder, and the two continued.

As the sun began to set and the long shadows lanced through the forest, Clarence could hear the faint and distant sound of dogs barking. They stopped. Goose's ears twisted up, and his body went rigid. He searched the distant forest for the sounds of his kin, and he knew they were near.

Clarence felt a chill run up his spine, and as he stood there, he felt a deep loneliness course through his body. In the vast panorama of the forest, across miles of trees and creeks, he was alone. No one would come save him or help him with what he was about to do. Fate rested entirely with him.

But as his mind began to spiral at the gravity of the moment and his insignificant presence in the world, he was wrenched from these thoughts by an undeniable sense of another. He turned and rested his eyes on Goose standing there beside him, his twitching nose still searching the forest. At that moment, the desolate void in Clarence's heart filled, and the cavernous darkness that grew within him like cancer drew closed. He could feel emotions welling inside him that he had not felt for years.

I am not alone.

I am not alone.

I am not alone.

The thought played in his mind over and over again. Goose looked up at him, his eyes alert and attentive. Clarence sensed that Goose could feel it too, and a faint smile drew across his weary face.

Clarence stepped toward Goose and bent down, setting one knee on the forest floor. He took the dog's large, bony face in his hands and leaned forward, placing his forehead against Goose's. For a long moment, the two rested like that in the forest, the warmth of their bodies reaching across the small span where their heads touched.

In the distance, the barking grew louder and frenzied. Clarence rose to his feet and looked through the forest.

You are not alone.

Then, they started forward through the woods once more. With each step, Clarence could feel the trees thinning, drawing them nearer and nearer to the barking. Soon, they reached the edge of the woods, and both studied the hollow. They could see shadows moving at the ends of chains. Behind the dogs, the mobile home lay dark, a rotting husk filled with many horrors. To the left, a soft yellow glow emanated from the rear windows of the house. The curtains were drawn tight, but Clarence could sense the Man was inside.

The two of them crept from the edge of the forest and hunkered down, slithering in the blackness to the edge of the hollow. When they reached the thin bushes where the tree line ended, they lay down. Clarence rolled on his back and pulled Goose close to him. Goose resisted for a moment, his eyes affixed on the clearing ahead of them. Finally, he relented and rested on the soft dirt next to Clarence.

Clarence lay there, breathing heavily. His heart raced, and he could feel beads of sweat forming on the back of his neck. He laid his head down on the cold ground and stared up into the darkened sky. Above him, a billion stars twinkled back.

CHAPTER 14

For a long while, the two of them lay in the tall grass at the edge of the woods. All around, fireflies flickered against the blackness. In the distance, Clarence could hear the shrill cries of the screech owl and the caterwauling of a mating fox. Before long, the biting flies descended, landing on the sweaty nape of his neck and the crown of his head. He brushed them away quietly and rubbed at the throbbing knots they left. Beside him, Goose lay prone, his eyes fixed on the clearing before them. The flies landed on his fur and prodded their stringers into his short coat, but he never flinched or withdrew his eyes from the place he once called home.

Occasionally, a chain rattled in the clearing ahead as one of the dogs adjusted their resting position in the dirt before the barrel or deep within. Goose's ears perked up each time, listening for further sounds, a whimper or whine or something to let him know who was there. After some time, he heard the telltale sounds of a chain dropping and hanging limp as a dog stood in the clearing. Goose lifted his eyes above the tall grass and searched the night for the shape.

There in the distance, he saw a familiar, stocky frame, the silhouette of thick muscles unmistakable in the darkness. Zeus stepped toward the center of the clearing in the direction where Goose and Clarence hid in the tall grass. Goose could see the faint twitching of his silhouette, and he knew he was searching the night sky with his nose. After a moment, he whined softly. Beside him, chains clinked deep in a blue barrel, and Goose knew it was Rocket, ferreted away in her hole far away from the world. Then, there was a rustle closer to them, and a familiar black shape slinked from the barrel and stood in the night, his nose twitching in the sky. Achilles.

The sight of his brother made Goose sit up in a tense crouch, ready to spring forward and run to the clearing. Clarence sensed him and rolled quickly on his stomach and placed his hand on Goose's back.

"No, no, no…" he whispered in somewhat of a panic, startled at the sudden commotion. Clarence could feel the tension leave Goose's body, and he relaxed slightly but never turned his gaze from the clearing.

Achilles whimpered anxiously; he sensed something. Zeus stepped forward on his chain, pulling it taut, and his nose rose high into the skin. Deep in his barrel, Rocket whined a manic, low whine as if fighting the urge to leave the barrel and explore the source of the sounds.

Clarence rubbed his hand up and down Goose's back, reassuring him in a whisper. "I know, friend. I know," was all he said. And he did.

When he was comfortable that Goose had settled, Clarence rolled on his back and rested his head in the tall grass. The blades shrouded his vision of the night sky, and for a moment, he lay in solitude with his thoughts. He breathed deeply several times, lowering his eyes and watching his chest rise and fall. Consciously, he exhaled through his nose, calming himself. All around him, the night grew still and quiet. After several long minutes, Clarence sat up slightly in the grass and gathered himself.

He reached beside him and grasped the cold wooden stock of the rifle and allowed it to warm in his hand. With the other hand, he reached down and opened the slide just slightly, a flash of copper visible in the chamber in the moonlight. Then he closed it again and shut his eyes for a moment.

He could feel Goose watching him now, and he

opened his eyes and turned to greet the dog. He reached out with his free hand and rubbed Goose affectionately behind the ear. Goose dipped his head slightly into his hand but kept one eye on the clearing above.

"I want you to wait here," said Clarence, knowing Goose had no reason to understand him. "I'm going to go take care of this," he said, his voice quivering. Goose began to rise as if following Clarence's command to come with him. Clarence rested his hand on Goose's back once more and pressed him gently down. "No," he said in a firm whisper. Clarence pointed at the ground. "You stay here."

Goose stood in a half crouch for a moment, the muscles of his legs quivering. His eyes stared into Clarence for what felt like an eternity, and finally, he lowered himself to the ground with a soft huff. Clarence stroked his back, reassuring him. "I promise I'll be back," he said, sounding unsure.

With that, he leaned forward and rose, hunched over, and gathered the rifle. In the clearing, the chains jingled again, and Goose tensed. Clarence scurried away from the clearing toward the wood line. His heart raced and the thousands of knots on his scalp and neck pulsed in pain.

When he reached the safety of the woods, he moved behind the thick trunk of a tree and braced himself, looking back into the clearing. In the tall grass, he could see a light spot and he knew that was Goose, just where he had left him, but he could sense the dog looking back at him. He took one last look at the dog and sent thoughts of affection into the night and then hurried away into the woods, circling the clearing toward the small house.

Soon, he reached the edge of the clearing where the woods met the rugged dirt road that led to the front of the house. To his right, the dingy house stood in the shadows. The unnatural yellow of a dangling porchlight illuminated the front of the house enough to reflect long slivers of paint peeling from its sides. To the left of the door, a ramshackle wooden bench sat, the slats of its backrest broken like jagged teeth. Clarence scanned the house for any movement. The black windows looked back, and he watched the tattered curtains for any signs of life but saw none. He glanced into the driveway and saw the shape of a battered, old pickup truck. He knew the Man was here. He crouched behind a tree at the edge of the forest and lifted the rifle up to his side, resting his hand on the bolt. His mind raced, and his heart pounded in his chest. He took a deep breath and studied the contour of the driveway that would lead him to the house.

A hundred yards away, Goose lay in the tall grass, his attention fixed on the clearing. He had watched Clarence move away until his shape vanished into the forest, and now, his eyes were drawn back to the dogs before him on their chains and in their barrels.

Then, he heard it. Somewhere off to his right, opposite from the way the man had gone, he heard a pained whimper, barely audible even in the silent night. His ears perked, and he listened again but heard nothing. His muscles tensed. He knew he had heard it. He lifted himself taller in the grass and twisted his keen ears toward where he had heard the sound.

He waited.

Nothing.

Goose rose to a crouch, and slowly, he sifted his way through the tall grass in the opposite direction of the house. Occasionally, he would stop and lift his head, his nose searching the air for any scents. He moved through the grass methodically for a long time, stopping and sniffing the air every thirty or forty feet. After a while, he heard nothing and smelled nothing and thought of turning back, but he pressed forward in the direction of the sound. After a few more paces, the rotten stench of festering wounds filled his nostrils like an unwelcome memory. The hackles rose on his back, and he moved forward cautiously, the scent growing stronger and stronger. As he drew near, he could hear a tiny whimper, the faintest sounds of life. Then, he saw the shimmer where the tall grass was slicked with blood.

In the silvery moonlight, he saw Queen lying there. Her coal-black body rested deep in the tall, blood-soaked grass. Goose looked upon her still, motionless body. Finally, he noticed her side rise almost imperceptibly and then fall slowly, a faint wheezing exhale from her nose blew the blades of grass. Her eyes were closed, and she didn't know Goose was there. He approached cautiously and studied her mangled body. Lying on her right side, he could see her left ear was nearly torn from her skull and dangled grotesquely. Blood bubbled gently from several holes near her shoulder.

Goose circled cautiously in the grass until he could see her face. When he reached her, he stopped in his tracks. The lips around her snout were torn away, revealing broken teeth and bloody gums. Goose could hear the air pressing through the fluid that filled her mouth. Once again, he saw her chest rise ever so slightly and then fall and rest still for a long moment before it rose again.

Then, she sensed him and opened her one eye that faced the night sky, her other buried deep into the grass. Her gaze shimmered in the night as she looked at him, seemingly the only part of her body that hadn't been torn and shredded. She stared at

Goose unblinking, and he looked back at her with pity. The tension left his body, and he lay down beside her in the tall grass. She was no threat to him now. She watched him helplessly as he rested beside her.

As he settled into the grass beside her, he whimpered, letting her know he was with her. She blinked once, surrendering herself to him. He whimpered again.

I will not hurt you

Queen blinked once and then closed her eye. Summoning all her energy, she inhaled deeply and then let out a long breath. The warm air blew across Goose's paws, and he could feel the bloody spittle stick to his fur.

Then, she opened her eye once more and looked at him. As she lay dying in the quiet black night, finally unbound by chains or touched by the cruel hands of men, their souls connected there in the tall grass of the hollow. After several minutes, Queen's eye grew weary, and Goose knew she was fading. She looked at him one last time, and he could feel the peacefulness within her. Then, her tired eye closed slowly, and she breathed out one final time. As the blades of grass wavered in the quiet night, she passed from the world, finally free of her torment.

Far away, just as Clarence was about to step on

the porch, the curtains on the front door suddenly flailed wildly as the tattered screen door flew open towards him. He jumped back, the rifle nearly slipping from his grip. The silent night split with the sound of gunfire as a white flash erupted in the doorway. Clarence staggered backward, the bullet slamming into his shoulder and sending him spinning. Another flash erupted and splintered the tattered wood on the post that held the dilapidated porch together.

Clarence spun backward, struggling to keep his feet beneath him. In his peripheral vision, he could see the jagged, rusted corner of the pickup truck looming closer as he staggered backward out of control. He pressed off with his foot and propelled himself sideways, landing hard on the ground with a thud. His vision exploded into bright lights as his neck whipped and his head cracked on the ground. With every ounce of strength he could muster, he clutched the rifle as he crashed to the ground. For a brief second, he lay there in the darkness, fighting to remain conscious. He opened his eyes just in time to see a wiry figure spring from the door of the house and charge at him, a black pistol clutched tightly in his outstretched hand.

Instinctively, Clarence lifted the rifle with his good arm, and he pulled on the trigger. The rifle recoiled and flew from his hands. The shot sailed just to the right of the charging figure and shattered a window of the house. Glass rained from the sky and sprayed across the front porch. The figure drew closer, and shadows loomed over Clarence. He looked up into the Man's twisted, snarling face.

"You don't belong here!" he glowered menacingly, the sweat dripping from his furrowed brow. His right arm raised the pistol, and Clarence could no longer see his face, only the endless pit of the gun barrel. Time seemed to slow, the world around went silent, and Clarence could see the muscles tense on the Man's forearm. He could feel the gun tilt just slightly as the Man began to squeeze the trigger.

Clarence began to close his eyes, but then, from his right, he could hear the heavy pounding of paws thudding urgently toward him across the hard dirt. He couldn't see it, but he could envision the muscles deeply knotted and surging forward with every ounce of energy they could bear. As the finger squeezed on the trigger, a blur of buckskin filled Clarence's vision followed by the thunderous sound of flesh and bone slamming into each other. A brilliant flash exploded from the muzzle of the gun just as it flew from the Man's hand into the tall grass beside the porch while he tumbled over violently. On the ground beside him, Goose tucked and rolled on his shoulder, spun, and was on his feet in the blink of an eye, crouched low and baring his teeth at the Man, who lay face down in the dirt in a heap.

Nearby, Clarence lay on his back in the hard dirt. Blood seeped from an open wound just below his left shoulder and soaked into the ground. His eyes fluttered as the blackness of night alternated rapidly with the pale white of infinity. He could feel Goose beside him, and he could sense the dog's tension. He opened his mouth to call to him, but his breath was faint, and he could not muster any words.

The darkness fell upon him, and his eyes closed deeply as he began to fade. In the distance, he could hear sirens approaching, and just as he lost consciousness, he heard tires crunching the gravel behind him.

CHAPTER 15

Swaddled in the blackness, Clarence wasn't aware of the array of tubes and wires that connected him to the incessantly bleeping machines on their cold metal stands. The hospital room was sterile and bland. Beside his bed, the nightstand and small wooden desk were barren of any personal touches—no flowers, cards, or handwritten notes. The room looked much as it did when they wheeled him in after surgery.

Nurses regularly entered the room to adjust knobs on the machines and scribble notes on various charts that hung from the foot of the bed. Occasionally, they whispered to the doctors, who periodically stepped just a few feet into the room to observe him, their demeanor as rigid as the white coats they wore.

But beneath the blanket of darkness that separated Clarence from the world of the living, thoughts and remembrances swirled like a thousand galaxies. Outwardly, his body lay rigid, tucked beneath a thin cotton covering, but inwardly, visions and memories of his life flooded his mind.

He saw himself standing before a large class of students in a neatly pressed plaid shirt. Their curious, young faces peered back at him from the raised rows of semi-circular tables. They sat enraptured at his lecture with pens in hands, fingers on laptop keys, and ears closely attuned to his every word. He reveled in their inquisitiveness and their eager chatter before each class. Each flourish of his marker on the whiteboard brought a flurry of typing, and every question he posed drew a dozen hands raised high.

The visions churned, and he saw himself at home in the small, quaint cottage in the quiet neighborhood not far from campus. He stood at the long, granite counter in the kitchen, pouring an espresso from the tidy black and silver machine that whirred and steamed. He could smell the hints of roasted almonds and hazelnuts. Just out the window, the neighbor's small, shaggy dog yipped faintly then darted playfully through the freshly fallen leaves.

From the other room, footsteps approached, and he turned to greet her. Loretta's effortless grace never ceased to amaze him. Her blonde hair glowed in the light that beamed through the house's tall windows. She stood in the doorway and smiled at him, and he felt her love. He rested his mug on the counter and went to greet her, and they embraced. Her hair caressed his bare cheek like lengths of silk.

"I love you," she said tenderly.

He turned until his lips were on her ear, and he whispered to her. "I love you forever."

She squeezed him tightly.

The clouds swirled and roiled, and the memory was gone. He stepped down the wide concrete steps of the old brick building that houses his office into the warm glow of post lights that illuminated the walkway before him. Beneath his arm, he clutched the binder of notes that had drawn him back here from the cottage. The night was calm and quiet; the gentle tread of his steps on the sidewalk was the only sound as he walked to his car. He started the engine and began the slow, meandering drive through campus on the way to the cottage. His mind drifted to the writing that would occupy him until late into the night.

He passed the rows of quaint brick buildings and wide, leafy trees that dotted the bucolic grounds and approached the small lake at the edge of campus. As he did, he noticed a sheriff's car parked in the shadows of a large oak, an unusual sight for this quiet place. Set deep in these rural hills, safety issues were rare on campus, and there was hardly ever a need for the sheriff, especially in this quiet area at this time of night.

He slowed as he drove past and glanced inconspicuously toward the vehicle. From the driver's seat, Deputy Hinton turned and glared back at him, his face twisted into a scowl.

As he passed, Clarence's eyes caught a glimpse of familiar golden locks in the seat beside Hinton. The soft glow of the post light illuminated her face as she turned toward him; her eyes drew wide, and her hand rose to cover her mouth.

The clouds in his mind churned again, and he saw himself sitting before Dean Kramer's imposing oak desk. The cold, ornate armrests of his stiff chair felt cold and callous. He was tired and disheveled. The sour stench of alcohol emanated from his clothes, and his face was sheepish. His attempts to look presentable had miserably failed, and he knew it.

Before him, Dean Kramer looked sullen; the disappointment was unmistakable on his deeply weathered face. Beside Dean Kramer, the university's Legal Counsel, a much younger man, stood rigidly with his arms folded across his chest. He could see their mouths moving but could not hear the words. Dean Kramer looked down at the desk as he slid a paper forward for him to sign. He could feel the pen wobbling in his hand, and Dean Kramer nodded for him to leave.

The visions swirled again, and he could see Loretta's big blue eyes beyond the threshold of the cottage, large tears welling in the corners, the type of tears that said, "Goodbye."

For three days, the memories ebbed and flowed through Clarence's mind as he lay comatose on the hospital bed. On the fourth day, he opened his eyes and stared blankly at the ceiling. The crisp chill of the room's air conditioner and the thousands of tiny peaks and valleys in the clean white stucco ceiling tiles grasped tightly to his consciousness and held it firm, pressing the memories into the deep corners of his mind.

The nurses and doctors came quickly to his bedside. They moved hurriedly in and out of the room at first, and he could hear them whispering in the hallway. Before long, they hovered over him, asking countless questions and pricking his veins with needles.

After a bustle of activity that seemed to take the better part of a day, they left, and the room fell silent for only a short time. Soon, the gaggle of doctors and nurses was replaced by new visitors. Clarence could hear the clicking of their boots on the hallway tile and could see their long shadows drawing closer just beyond the door.

THE DOG IN THE HOLLOW

Sheriff Jefferson entered the room slowly and stood beside his bed. Several paces behind him, Deputy Hinton stood uncomfortably.

"I'm glad to see you pulled through, Clarence," said Jefferson. His words were flat and lacked emotion. Clarence mustered only a nod. His mouth was dry, and he had little desire to speak, especially to these two.

Jefferson paused for a moment. Hinton shifted on his feet behind him and placed his thumbs into his belt loops.

"We owe you a debt of gratitude, Clarence," said Jefferson somewhat meekly. "I thought I'd come up here myself and tell you." He looked as if he was waiting for a reaction from Clarence, who only looked stared back at him blankly.

Jefferson glanced over his shoulder at Hinton and then spoke again. "Virgil Pickens is a bad man, Clarence." He paused again, looking down, and then continued, "I know your concern was those dogs, but there's a lot more to it than that."

Hinton looked up, gauging Clarence's reaction. There was none.

Jefferson continued, "As things would have it, he's got warrants out of Kentucky—murder, drugs, racketeering…a whole host of terrible things," he said, his inflection rising at the end.

Slowly, the words began to penetrate

Clarence's stupor, and his face must have shown something resembling surprise.

"We were just as surprised," responded Jefferson. "We never would've known he was living right under our noses if you hadn't led us to him."

Clarence's lips parted to speak. The words came very slowly. "How…did…you find me?" he asked, his voice barely a whisper.

Jefferson studied him for a moment. "Margaret came and told us. Said you were going to do something crazy. She pleaded with us to go find you."

Clarence's eyes looked away for a moment, and he studied the knitted white blanket splayed over his feet. It was only then that he remembered why he lay here in this hospital bed. He glanced to his left and at the sight of the heavy bandage on his shoulder. For the first time since he woke, he could feel the pain throbbing through his body.

Jefferson watched him closely. "You're a lucky man, Clarence. A few inches the other way and we wouldn't be sitting here having this conversation," he said, his eyes moving up and down Clarence's heavy bandages.

Clarence stared at the textures on the white gauze that swaddled his arm and shoulder. He reached inward to replay the scene that brought him here. The white flash of the muzzle filled his mind and made him shudder. He could feel the heat from the barrel and the spray of gunpowder. Then, he could hear flesh and bone colliding above him as he waited to die. He jerked his head up and looked urgently at Jefferson.

"Where is Goose?" he demanded. His voice was suddenly strong.

Jefferson looked back at him, and his face grew solemn. Behind him, Hinton shuffled, looking down at the ground.

"The dog?" asked Jefferson. He paused for a moment, studying Clarence's face. "I don't know, Clarence," he said and broke Clarence's gaze.

Clarence's heart sank, and his chest brimmed with fury. "You don't know?!" he demanded. "Is he alive?"

Jefferson looked down at the tile floor. "I really don't know, Clarence," he said, lifting his gaze just slightly to greet Clarence's. "He ran off into the woods when we pulled up. Lights and sirens must've spooked him. No one's seen him since."

Clarence rested back and stared at the ceiling. He could feel his heart racing.

"I know what he meant to you, and I can promise you that we've been keeping an eye out for him. Hinton's been up in those woods twice now with a group looking for him." He nodded over his shoulder at Hinton, who stood with his head bowed.

Clarence's heartbeat pounded in his ears. He tried to sit up in bed, but a dagger of pain shot down his arm, and he fell back on the mattress, wincing and moaning. He opened his eyes and looked back at Jefferson. "The others? Where are they?" he demanded.

Jefferson was quiet for a long moment, and then shook his head slowly. "They're gone, Clarence," he said.

On the far wall, the air conditioner whirred to life.

"They were just too aggressive. Animal Control had to put them down." He feigned a slight frown.

Clarence's breath caught in his throat, and he could feel himself starting to choke. He sat up and gasped for air. Jefferson stepped forward and placed a hand on Clarence's back to comfort him then looked over his shoulder and called out for a nurse.

Clarence leaned back in the bed, still gasping and eyes rolled backward. It was too much to take, and the room started to fade to black. He could hear the nurse's feet rushing in, and he watched her brush Jefferson and Hinton away as she hurried to the bedside. "All right officers, your talk is over. Mr. Crandall needs his rest," she told them, her tone prickly.

For two more days, Clarence lay in the hospital bed, his mind singularly occupied with thoughts of Goose. It was undeniable that the dog was tough, and Clarence was sure he could survive a few days in the woods. But how would he ever find him? Could he make his way to the cabin? What if Hinton found him first and killed him like the others because he was "too aggressive"? What would he eat, and where would he drink? Was he injured or even shot by Pickens?

Clarence pleaded with the nurses to help him out of bed so he could find Goose. When that failed, he begged with them for any word on the search for the dog but never heard any.

And so he lay there in bed, staring up at the ceiling, alone with his thoughts. Finally, the doctor told him there was no sign of infection, and he would probably be released later that day. They sent in a social worker—a friendly, shorter woman with cherub cheeks and straight gray bangs. She talked quietly and gently to Clarence as if the slightest noise would shatter him to pieces. She asked him where he lived, whether he had family he could stay with, whether he had the means to care for himself.

Clarence said only what was needed to appease her and invite no further attention. She seemed skeptical but said she would not impede his release and wished him well, giving him her card should he ever need assistance. Clarence folded the card and stuffed it in the crack between the bed frame and the mattress.

"What time am I being released?" he asked the nurse, somewhat impatiently as she stood making notes on a chart at the foot of his bed.

She looked up without lifting her head. "Soon, Mr. Crandall," she said curtly. "The doctor needs to add notes to your discharge paperwork and fill a prescription."

Clarence said nothing further. His mind raced back to the forest, and he began to think of all the places he would search for Goose. He looked out the windows and studied the sky, hoping they would release him before the sun set, but he resolved to search through the night if necessary.

Soon, the nurse finished her notes and left. Before long, he heard footsteps in the hall. They were slow and measured, and he could hear the trepidation in their steps. A thin shadow loomed just outside the door, and Clarence sat up eagerly in bed to greet the doctor who would discharge him.

Then, he saw her in the doorway, and his breath left him once again.

She entered timidly and approached with her head bowed, the flaxen hair covering her face.

THE DOG IN THE HOLLOW

Slowly, she lifted her eyes and looked at him; her piercing blue eyes were filled with emotion.

"Hello, Clarence" was all she said softly, but the words carried so much more.

For a long moment, Clarence could not speak. His face was blank, but the tides of emotion brewed deep within him. Finally, he mustered a word. "Loretta," was all he could say.

In a tentative silence, they looked upon each other, sensing what the other was feeling.

"May I come closer?" she asked gently.

Clarence nodded quickly, almost before she finished. "Yes, yes. Of course," he said. After everything, he still longed for her.

She clasped her hands together before her and approached the side of the bed until she was standing next to him. He seemed to draw energy from the sweet hint of her perfume. Her eyes scanned the bandages on his shoulder, and she leaned forward to tug at the blanket, pulling it up delicately to cover him. She reached out and took his hand.

Her touch pulsed through his body like electricity, and Clarence felt intoxicated. It had been a long time since he had felt her hand. He squeezed gently and could feel the warmth radiating between the two of them.

"I'm proud of you, Clarence," she said tenderly

as she studied him.

Clarence looked down. The emotions were almost too intense. He said nothing. There was a long pause. He could tell she was thinking deeply about what would come next.

"And I'm sorry, Clarence," she said…finally. It was the first time he'd heard those words, and they stabbed his heart, tearing open old wounds long-sealed with bitterness.

"I'm so sorry for everything that happened." She squeezed his hand tightly and stared down at the ground, a tear forming in her eye.

Clarence looked away and focused on the shape of his feet tucked tightly into the blanket. Around him, the world seemed to spin, and he felt nauseous. He had not expected this.

She looked back at him, her eyes almost pleading now. "Why don't you come, Clarence?" she said. Her tone was warm and hopeful. "Come back and be part of the town, part of this community."

He stared ahead, absorbing her words.

"I bet the university will take you back. You're a hero now, Clarence," she said, her tone lifting.

The words stung him. He never wanted to be a hero. He never sought the adoration of those who viewed him as a pariah.

Loretta sensed the depth of his thoughts. "Will

you think about it, Clarence?" she said. "We can get you a loft above the shops. I'll help you, Clarence. Let me help you for what I've done." She stroked his arm. "Please come back from the woods, Clarence. You deserve this."

Clarence gazed unblinking at his feet beneath the blanket. His mind wandered to his cabin on the mountaintop, the thin mattress on the old wire frame that made his joints ache in the morning, the soggy nights when mosquitos would wiggle through the cracks and sting him beneath the thin covers, the rain from mountain storms that would trickle through the roof and leave small puddles on the dirt floor. He thought of the long walks to town in his worn shoes, the throbbing in his muscles as he carried sacks of groceries for miles back up the hill to the shack. The jeers of students mocking him as he shambled through town rang in his ears.

His thoughts wandered to happier times when he felt whole and filled with purpose. He longed for the rigors of academia, the late-night research beneath the soft glow of his desk lamp, the exhilaration of publishing a new scholarly paper, the stimulating hours spent debating theory with colleagues. He missed the vibrance of the students with their engaging expressions and rich questions. He could smell the aroma of warm espresso steaming up from his coffee cup as he sat at the shop counter and chatted casually with the workers and students.

She squeezed his hand softly, and he could sense her gaze on him. The clouds churned, and his thoughts shifted to the forest; the trees splayed out in his vision all along the horizon. He could hear the calls of the Whippoorwill, the gentle crunch of leaves as raccoons and muskrats foraged nearby, the brisk night sky peppered with infinite stars that hung high above. And somewhere out there, he could see him—hungry and tired and longing for nothing more than his pile of blankets in the corner and his person nearby, reading quietly in the candlelight.

Finally, he lifted his head and squeezed Loretta's hand weakly. "Thank you, Loretta." A faint smile crossed his face. "It means a lot that you came here."

She smiled warmly at him.

He gazed into her blue eyes, savoring long-forgotten memories, and said nothing for a moment.

Then he spoke. "The woods are my home now."

Clarence swung the car door closed, and his feet shuffled on the strewn gravel of the emergency lane beside the mountain road. With an electric thrum, the window rolled down. He leaned over and peered inside the car. Margaret looked back at him, an expression of deep concern on her face.

"Thank you, Margaret," he said and gave her a kind smile. "I owe you more than you know. For everything." He meant it.

Margaret lowered her weary eyes and nodded faintly. "I'll worry about you, Clarence," she said, looking down at the floorboard. "But I believe in you, whatever you do," she added as she looked up at him.

Clarence could feel a tear welling in the corner of his eye and quickly pressed it away with his knuckle. "That means a lot," he replied, his voice quivering slightly.

They looked upon each other in silence there on the roadside, a light drizzle falling into Clarence's thick hair. Feet away, cars and trucks sped by, kicking up a grimy spray of mud and road dust.

"Take care of yourself, Clarence. I'm here if you need me." She looked him in the eye to make sure he understood. "And I hope you find him."

Clarence nodded solemnly, and a tear snuck out of his eye and rolled down his cheek. He mustered a false smile. Then Margaret rolled up the window, and the orange glow of her blinker cast a faint light against the darkening forest. Clarence stepped back from the roadside and watched her pull away.

WILL LOWREY

He turned and faced the deep woods that spanned out before him and cinched his backpack over his good shoulder. Beneath the raincoat Margaret had brought for him, his other shoulder was still bandaged heavily but no longer ached. As night fell, he started into the forest, alone.

Guided by the beam of a single flashlight, he journeyed miles into the woods and up the mountainside, enveloped by the trees. All around him, the denizens of the forest greeted him with a chorus of whirrs, chirps, and distant howls.

In the darkness, Clarence reached the shack. To his relief, everything looked intact, and the door was closed firmly. He stood on the threshold of the cabin and looked out into the dark woods for any sign of Goose. He wouldn't admit it to himself, but deep down, he had lost hope. Even if Goose could find his way to the cabin, there was no one there to greet him or feed him or fluff his blankets at night. The dog might have come and sniffed around for a day or two—if he was even still alive—but he would surely have moved on for the next hand to feed and comfort him. That's just the way the world worked.

Then, deep within the black cloak of the forest, Clarence heard a familiar *yip yip*.

He stepped down from the threshold and faced the direction of the sound. He held his breath and listened into the silence until he could hear the strange pattern of Fenton's three paws pressing into the ground and approaching. In the moonlight, he could faintly see his grayish-brown fur passing behind the black silhouettes of towering trees. As he always did, Fenton stood at a distance, his haunting gaze upon the man. For a long moment, the two stood there looking at each other, and for the first time in many days, Clarence felt some peace in the company of his wild friend.

Then, the stillness of the forest gave way to sounds of other footsteps, these less nimble and stealthy. The paws crunched hurriedly on the carpet of leaves, growing closer. Clarence could feel his spirit before he saw him, and his heart welled with emotion. His breath caught for a moment, and just then, the old familiar patch of buckskin emerged into the moonlit night.

Like some haggard mongrel reverted to primitive form, Goose stepped brusquely from the forest and stood with his mouth wide open, breathing hard. His coat was streaked with grime, and his paws were covered in black mud from the creek beds. He paused for a moment, panting heavily. His eyes scanned the clearing and finally fell upon the figure standing just before the cabin. Then, his mouth closed, and his body grew soft, the tension draining from him. Slowly, his tail began to wag side to side, and suddenly, he charged forward, galloping toward the man.

Tears pooled in Clarence's eyes and poured down his cheeks as he dropped to his knees and met Goose's wild charge. The dog barreled into his chest, and Clarence wobbled backward, wrapping the dog in a great embrace and pulling him tightly into himself as if they were one. He never noticed the throbbing in his shoulder. Goose twisted and contorted his bulky head, angling his mouth to bestow slobbery kisses on Clarence's face, which the man embraced while he wept.

Beneath the twinkling stars high above the forest, man and dog embraced and were whole once more.

"We're home," said Clarence softly through his tears.

And they were.

THANK YOU

Thank you for taking the time to read this book. If you found this reading worthwhile, please consider leaving a review wherever you purchased the book. More reviews will help more readers find and appreciate this story.

If you would like to explore my other books and receive a free short story based on the events of "Chasing the Blue Sky," please visit:

www.lomackpublishing.com

Thank you again for giving your valuable time to read this book. I hope you found the time well-spent.

~ Will Lowrey ~

ABOUT THE AUTHOR

WILL LOWREY is an attorney and animal rights advocate from Richmond, Virginia. He holds a Juris Doctor from Vermont Law School and a Bachelor of Science from Virginia Commonwealth University. For close to two decades, both before and after law school, Will has been actively involved in animal causes. His experiences include deployments to assist animals in disasters, the closure of roadside zoos, caring for animals from dog and cock fighting cases, community outreach for low-income pet owners in areas ranging from urban neighborhoods to Native American reservations, animal rights protests, animal sheltering, public records campaigns against large institutions conducting animal research, and countless other adventures.

In 2018, Will founded Lomack Publishing to promote the rights, interests, and dignity of animals through self-published literature. Will is also the author of "Chasing the Blue Sky," "Where the Irises Bloom," "Words on a Killing," "The Animals v. Samuel Willis," "Odd Robert," and "Once in a Wild" through Lomack Publishing as well as "We the Pit Bull: The Fate of Pit Bulls Under the United 170 States Constitution" published in the Lewis and Clark Animal Law Review Journal, Volume 24,

Issue 2.

While most of Will's writing focuses on animal causes, he has dabbled in other areas, writing "Simple Strategies for the Bar Exam," a guide for law students and attorneys taking the bar exam, as well as "The Tenebrous Mind," a collection of horror stories.

Will enjoys hearing from readers. If you'd like to contact him, please visit:

www.lomackpublishing.com

11417150R00119